MY
INDIAN

MI'SEL Joe

AND

SHEILA O'Neill

BREAKWA

Breakwater Books
P.O. Box 2188, St. John's, NL, Canada, A1C 6E6
www.breakwaterbooks.com

Cover artwork: *My Indian*, Prismacolor pencils on rag, by Jerry Evans
Author photos: Ritche Perez
Interior layout: Sarah Hansen

A CIP catalogue record for this book is available from Library and Archives Canada.

ISBN 978-1-55081-878-9 (softcover)

 Canada Council for the Arts Conseil des Arts du Canada Canadä Newfoundland Labrador

We acknowledge the support of the Canada Council for the Arts.
We acknowledge the financial support of the Government of Canada through the Department of Heritage and the Government of Newfoundland and Labrador through the Department of Tourism, Culture, Arts and Recreation for our publishing activities.

Printed and bound in Canada.

Breakwater Books is committed to choosing papers and materials for our books that help to protect our environment. To this end, this book is printed on a recycled paper and other sources that are certified by the Forest Stewardship Council®.

ACKNOWLEDGEMENTS

Thank you to Andrea MacDonald and the Board of Historic Sites Association of Newfoundland and Labrador for the writing grant; Robert Cuff, Gerald Penney (deceased) and Patricia Sandercock for research; Bill Brake, Parks Canada; Jerry Evans for artwork; Greg Jeddore for maps; Ritche Perez for author photos; Curtis Michael and Melvin Jeddore for language resources; Rebecca Rose, Jocelyne Thomas, Samantha Fitzpatrick, Rhonda Molloy and the incredible staff at Breakwater Books; Lisa Frenette for copyediting; Colletta Joe for editing and transcribing; and to all the people over the years who listened to Chief Joe talk about telling this story.

NOTE TO READERS

There are regional variations and dialects in the spoken (and sometimes written) languages of most cultures. The Mi'kmaw language and spellings used in this text are those of the Mi'kmaw Elders of Miawpukek First Nation.

TABLE OF CONTENTS

AFTERWORD

APPENDICES

SULIEWEY'S TALE

Chapter 1 → **THE DREAM**

The young warrior breathed in the minty scent of the witch hazel leaves being brushed over his skin by the Elders. The men were scenting his body and sensitizing his skin for the ceremony that was about to take place.

His body warmed from the heat of the Sweat Lodge; the soft leaves sounded like the wings of a thousand butterflies fluttering over his skin. The sound intensified after bear oil was rubbed onto his skin, and he could hear the beating wings of the kitpu as the Elders brushed his body over and over with the witch hazel branches.

His mind drifted as his senses were awakened, and he knew that across the river, the women were doing the same for his bride—preparing her for their marriage ceremony and for their first night in the Coming Together wiquom.

The women would dress his bride in a soft qalipu skin dress, decorated by the older women in the village, and her long black hair would be oiled with bear oil scented with wild roses and plants to make it shiny and fragrant. The men would dress him in qalipu skin leggings and jacket, made special for this day and bleached nearly pure white by the sun. On their feet, both would wear new qalipu skin moccasins, worn only this one time and then hung as a symbol of the beginning of their journey together.

Two streams come together and meet below the village. Two Sweat Lodges would be set up on either side of the encampment, one for the men and one for the women. The women would lead her to the centre of the encampment, as the men would lead him, through the archways of young birch and witch hazel saplings that covered their paths. There the Sacred Fire would be burning, and the clans would be gathered. The grandmothers and grandfathers would perform the Coming Together ceremony.

Blueberries and lu'skinikin—Indian bread—would be laid out on birchbark. First, the young warrior would feed his bride, and then she would feed him, symbolizing their commitment to feed each other's bodies and spirits—to care for and look after one another for all of time. He would then tie a white kitpu feather to his bride's hair as a sign of strength, courage, and purity. From then on, she would always wear it in her hair to show that she was a married woman and had gone through the marriage ceremony. She would then do the same for him, using a mature kitpu feather. He would collect many more kitpu feathers over his lifetime, but he would always wear this one feather as a sign of strength, courage, and maturity, and as a symbol of his union with his young bride.

The family of the young man would speak to the young woman's family: "This young man that we present to you will always be a protector and a provider for this young woman and her family. He has shown himself to be a good hunter and provider, and he will make a good husband and a good father for their children." Then the young woman's family would do the same: "This young woman that we present to you will make a good wife and have many children. She will keep your lodge comfortable and warm, and she will always look after you, take care of you, and be respectful of who we are and our ties to our culture and our land."

Clan Elders would mark their clan symbol on a piece of birchbark as witness to the ceremony. The young warrior would then dance around the Sacred Fire four times, singing the marriage chant. He and his bride would be presented with their journey stick and would be led to the wikuom to complete their Coming Together.

The wikuom would be prepared with a bed of qalipu skin—the dense hide of older qalipu on the bottom and the soft, young hide of yearling qalipu on the top to use as a cover. Witch hazel branches would be hung from strips of leather, low enough to brush gently over their skin as they lay together on the hides.

The young couple would enter the wikuom and pull the flap down. The village would then begin their celebration around the fire, dancing and singing long into the night and not stopping until the young couple came out of the wikuom at sunrise.

A baby would be conceived that night.

Chapter 2 → BIRTHING TIME

The warrior and his grandfather sat by the fire outside the wikuom, talking. They talked about their hunting season and the number of qalipu they'd brought home, dried, and put away in their storage. They talked about the eels and the salmon and the codfish they caught during the summer and how they were well provided for the winter months. They talked about how the young man had proven his capabilities as a hunter and a tracker, not only providing for his young wife who was expecting their first child, which was exciting, but also how he'd provided food for the entire village. Everyone in the village benefitted from his hard work. There were many salmon hanging on the drying rack along with eels and codfish; many quarters of qalipu meat; several furs from beaver, fox, and otter that they had caught; and the qalipu hide would be made into clothing, bedding, and used for the babiche—the snowshoe lacings.

They used all parts of the qalipu; nothing was ever wasted. They would cut the shanks to make skin boots for themselves. The qalipu leg has a natural heel, and this was saved to make the skin boots, over which they wore moccasins. Men made the shanks into boots in the camp; women made moccasins in the village.

While they were sitting there, waiting for the birth of the child, they talked of all these things. Every now and again, Grandmother would come out and talk in low tones to Grandfather. Grandfather would then come and tell the young man that everything was okay, that it was just taking a little longer than it normally would. There was no reason for concern.

As they waited, they made tea and cooked lu'skinikin over the fire and roasted qalipu meat for their lunch. From time to time, other members of the village would drop by and talk to them.

Suddenly, Grandmother came out of the birthing

lodge and said, "Lpa'tu'jij! You have a son!"

Normally, this name she called him—"Little Boy"—embarrassed him, but today he was too excited to mind.

Grandmother went back into the birthing lodge where she and the other women were looking after the new mother and her son. Finally, Lpa'tu'jij was permitted to enter the lodge and sit with his wife. The baby had coal black hair with a tiny streak of silver on the side of his head. When he was brought around to all the people in the village, everyone remarked about the silver streak. "Like his grandfather," they said. Thus, the Elders named him Suliewey—Silver. In later years, the missionaries would baptize him Sylvester.

There was great celebration in the village at the birth of this young Suliewey. Somehow, they all knew that this infant child, with the unusual streak of silver in his hair, would do things that were different.

Chapter 3 → GROWING UP ON THE LAND

Suliewey was used to being out on the land from a very young age. His grandfather made a cradleboard for him to be carried in, and as a young child his parents took him everywhere they went. As he grew, he followed his father, his uncles, and his grandfathers out on the land. He was present when they went after qalipu, and he helped them with the cleaning of the hides, making them ready for skin boots and clothing.

He also walked with his grandmother to pick medicines for use when someone was sick. She taught him what plants to pick to make the seven sorts of medicine. He never really knew he was learning those things; for him it was just fun to be out on the land. Suliewey learned all these things at an early age.

Suliewey grew up in a time when the land wasn't always kind, but everyone played a part in village life. Life wasn't always easy, but it was good. Everyone pitched in to make the village safe, strong, and friendly to everyone. He grew up in a time when there was famine and when there was feasting. If there wasn't very much food hanging on the smoke racks, then Suliewey knew that everyone was living the same way. But when there were lots, everyone came together and gave thanks for all that they had and all that they could get. They sat down together, not only to have a meal and to sit, pray, sing, and laugh, but also to think about the animals that gave up their lives so the people of the village could live. Every time a qalipu went down, they would stand over it, pray, and give thanks to the animal for giving up its life for them. It was the same with everything they caught, whether large or small; every living thing was given respect. When they walked on the land, they even avoided stepping on medicine plants that they recognized. And when they came to fresh, clean water—even a little stream—they gave a special prayer to give thanks for being able to kneel down and drink the cool water from it.

The lakes themselves had a special meaning. Not only did the lakes provide life to them, because water is life-giving, but lakes were also the routes of transportation. They provided fish, which was an important part of their diet. Around the lakes, there were different kinds of medicine from what one could find inland. They knew that if they watched the animals in the springtime, they would gravitate towards the lakes and the river bottoms; they knew that there would be different kinds of medicines and different kinds of food that they could use from those places. So, the animals played a big part in their lives.

Suliewey grew up in that time. The work was hard, but there was freedom and no thought of disagreements between nations; there was only survival, teaching your children, and teaching everyone that it takes all the people to become stronger and build a village where everyone is protected. Suliewey's education came from walking on the land and recognizing the simplest things, like how the juniper trees are pointed in the general direction of the east and could be used for wayfinding on the land.

Living on this island, he knew that some parts of some rivers ran to the east, some ran to the south, and some parts to the west. All young Mi'kmaw people were taught the language of the land. They were given the landmarks to recognize, so that when they were out there by themselves, they would know what to look for. Wayfinding was taught by using the stars. Should they be on the water, they could travel by looking at the stars. They also grew up knowing that the moon played an important part in their lives. The sun was an important part of their life too, of course; it helped things grow. But the moon played an important part in a different way. The moon told them when it was a good time to go hunting—when the animals were at their fattest and in the best shape. It also told them when it was a good time to go fishing—when the tide was at its highest or lowest. If you wanted to have good, dry wood, the best time to go cut it was based on the moon. If you cut it at the wrong time, it would never dry.

Suliewey learned from the land, even as he grew up on it. He became a part of the land; he smelled it on his skin, he felt it under his feet, and he slept on it at night. The land provided shelter and food, and he grew up learning to respect it and the gifts that it provided.

Chapter 4 ➔ **GRANDFATHER SPEAKS IN A STRANGE LANGUAGE**

Something awakened Suliewey from a sound sleep. The fire in his grandfather's wikuom had burned down to a few embers. Suliewey whispered to his grandfather and asked him if he was awake, but he did not reply.

It was then that Suliewey heard his grandfather talking to someone very softly. He rubbed his eyes to clear them of sleep so that he could see who had come to visit while he was sleeping. His grandfather was sitting by the fire with his back to Suliewey, and he could not see the face of his grandfather's friend.

There was something strange about the conversation. The person who spoke to Grandfather did so in a different language, yet Grandfather seemed to understand what was being said. Suliewey wondered if he should put some more wood on the fire, but there seemed to be something stopping him from doing so.

Suliewey tried to understand what was being said as he snuggled down in his bed of qalipu skin. As he looked out through the smoke hole, he could see it was still dark. Who could this person be that Grandfather was speaking with?

He must have fallen asleep then, because when he opened his eyes again, a new day had come and Grandfather was moving around outside. "Come and eat," Grandfather said as he moved the fire coals. "You must eat fast because today we move to the Sacred Mountain."

"Who did you speak with last night?" Suliewey asked.

Grandfather looked at him with surprise. "Did you hear?" he asked. He then turned toward the mountain, and even though Suliewey saw his lips move, no words could be heard.

"Grandfather must be praying," he thought to himself, but Grandfather had such a troubled look on his face that Suliewey did not think that this could be so.

"What is troubling you, Grandfather?" he asked.

"When the time is right, we will talk," Grandfather replied. Just at that moment, a qalipu came out of the woods and was heading for the camp.

"Are you going to kill the qalipu, Grandfather?" Suliewey asked.

"No," said Grandfather. "We have plenty of food, and to kill such a fine animal for sport would upset the animal spirit and our luck will always be bad. We must leave for the mountain today; the answers I seek can only be found there."

The sun had only been up for a short time when they started to walk across the big bog toward the mountain. It looked so close with the fog hanging around its top. As the morning wore on, the fog cleared, and they could see the mountaintop more clearly. Grandfather stopped and waited for young Suliewey, and then he pointed out the spot to which they were headed. It looked like a small black spot on the side of the mountain. "That is where the little people live," Grandfather said. "The Wuklatmu'jk."

"I don't think I want to go any further," Suliewey replied, fearful of the little people. "I'll go back to our wikuom. Our wikuom is much nearer than that big mountain."

"Don't be afraid. The little people are our friends, and we will leave them gifts," Grandfather replied.

"But Grandfather, will they not be angry because we disturb them?" Suliewey asked.

"No," said Grandfather. "We have been invited to talk to them, and it is a long way off. We have many miles yet to go."

As they headed off toward the mountain, Grandfather suddenly stopped at the top of a small hill and went down on one knee, making a motion for his grandson to be quiet. Suliewey crept forward to where his grandfather was kneeling, trying to see what he was looking at, but every time he moved Grandfather gave him a look and put his finger to his lips. "Be quiet," he whispered.

After what seemed like hours, Grandfather moved back toward Suliewey and whispered to him. "We will go back down the hill," he said.

"BUT GRANDFATHER..."

"Be quiet," he whispered, and he moved off down the hill in the same way they had come up just a few minutes ago.

When they reached the edge of the woods, they stopped and sat down. By this time, Suliewey was so curious as to what had made his grandfather turn back that he was bursting with a hundred questions. Finally, Grandfather said, "On the other side of the hill were some of our brothers from the north and they looked like they were also heading for the Sacred Mountain."

"Will they harm us, Grandfather?" Suliewey asked.

"I do not think so, my son," he answered. "We have not been at war, but they are on our territory."

"But why would they be heading for the Sacred Mountain?" Suliewey asked. Grandfather did not answer. It was the first time Suliewey had seen his grandfather look worried about anything.

After a while, they went back to the hill. As they neared the top, they crept very slowly, using every bit of cover that was there. Suliewey heard his grandfather give a sigh of relief when he saw that there was no one on the other side.

As they walked on, they crossed the tracks of the Beothuk. There were three people in the party. Grandfather studied their tracks for a while and then he said, "We must follow their tracks, because that is the only path to the mountain."

All day as they walked, Grandfather kept a lookout for the people from the north. Suliewey wondered what they were like, as he knew from their tracks that one of them was about his size. *Were they watching us or afraid of us? Would they make good friends for me?* he wondered.

As Suliewey walked along, daydreaming about becoming friends with the Beothuk, he forgot to keep up with Grandfather; he was nowhere in sight. *The Beothuk will get me now for sure,* he thought. He had visions of being roasted over the fire or being a slave to the Beothuk people for the rest of his life. Throwing his bundle on the ground, he started to run, screaming at the top of his voice: "Grandfather! Please wait for me!"

Suliewey ran through the woods, until he came to a giant pine tree. Fifty feet away, his grandfather sat, smoking his pipe with a smile on his face as wide as a river's mouth. Just seeing his smile again made Suliewey forget all about being scared. Grandfather said, "We should never be ashamed to be afraid. Now go back and get your bundle, and then we can talk." When Suliewey returned, grandfather told him stories about how many times he had been afraid. Looking at his grandfather, who stood over six feet tall, Suliewey could not imagine him ever being afraid of anything.

After resting for a while, they again started to walk. Grandfather's bundle looked so big that he almost looked like some strange beast with a great lump on his back. The closer they got to Pmaqtin, the Sacred Mountain, the more worried Grandfather looked. He seemed to be looking in every direction at once, but Suliewey was confused. The people from the north were still somewhere ahead of them. Was that why Grandfather was worried? The young boy wished they would stop soon because his feet were sore from all the walking, and his moccasins were wet and had holes in the bottom. "Grandfather, how long now since we had breakfast?" he asked, not really wanting to let him know that he was hungry and tired.

After a little while, Grandfather said, "We will stop soon. Just across this barren is a nice stream where we will catch some trout for our lunch. I know you are not tired, because you are young and strong, but your poor old grandfather is getting old and weak and cannot walk from dawn to when the sun is in the middle of the sky." At that minute, Suliewey could have walked until the sun had sunk in the trees to the west. He would have walked by Grandfather, his chest stuck out, had he not looked and seen a teasing little smile on Grandfather's face. Suliewey smiled back at him, and Grandfather looked happier than his grandson had seen him in a long time. "You make the fire now and I will get our lunch," he said.

As Suliewey gathered the wood for the fire, he wondered why they had left their camp down by the ocean. Did the stranger Grandfather spoke with last night have something to do with their sudden move to the mountain?

Soon there was a nice fire going, so he lay back on the fine sand to wait for Grandfather's return, but he must have fallen asleep because the next thing he knew, Grandfather was shaking him. "Wake up, boy. The fish are cooked, and if you don't want it, the bears will come and eat it."

Grandfather had lu'skinikin cooking; he rolled dough around a long stick and placed it near the flames, while two big brook trout were roasting over the fire. Suliewey wished they could stay there forever.

After they had eaten, Grandfather lit up his stone pipe. It was so quiet and peaceful. "Do you think the Beothuk boy is bigger than me, Grandfather?" Suliewey asked.

"I don't know, but he is probably just as afraid of getting lost as you are," Grandfather replied.

"I wonder why they are going to our Sacred Mountain."

Grandfather did not reply, but he began to look around again as if there was someone watching them from the trees. "It's getting late. We will have to find a campsite before dark."

That night at campfire, after they had made a shelter and cooked a supper of qalipu meat, Grandfather said, "I have to tell you a story, Suliewey. This happened a long time ago, and not a lot of people know about this story except some of the older people in our village.

"We were all out as a family, gathering berries for our winter food, and my grandmother told me not to wander too far away from where everybody was picking berries. And I forgot, and I wandered too far away, and I realized I was so far away from everyone else that I wasn't quite sure how to get back to where the berry pickers were.

"I came across a small stream and my feet were starting to hurt, so I took off my moccasins and I soaked my feet in the stream to cool them off, and I took a cold drink of water. I was laying back on the grass beside the stream remembering what my grandfather always told me: If you wander away, look at your surroundings and always look back in the direction you come from so that you will know your way back. My grandfather also said that if you find that you have lost your way, stay where you are and we will find you.

"I was only a lpa'tu'jij, maybe six years old. I was almost asleep when I had a sense that there was someone nearby. I opened my eyes, thinking that it would be my grandfather looking for me. But there was a very large man, and he was covered in red ochre. He just stood there staring at me for the longest time. Then he picked me up and put me over his shoulder and started walking. It didn't matter how much I screamed and kicked, he just held on and kept walking.

"After what seemed like a long time, we came to an encampment. And it was an encampment of people— Red Indians. They brought me to the centre of the village and put me down. I immediately started to run, but I was encircled by women and children and men who looked at me and talked to me in a language that I didn't understand. Some of the women came and fed me; they put me in one of their wikuoms with some children and older women, and they kept an eye on me all night.

"Early the next morning they left the campsite and took me with them. We travelled for days and days. I kept trying to tell them I wanted to go and find my family, but no one seemed to understand what I was saying. And we kept walking. We came to a mighty river and along the riverbanks there were gwitn—funny-looking canoes that were different than ours, which were made from birchbark and called maskwiey gwitn. And we went upriver. It seemed to me like it was weeks and weeks.

"When we got to their campsite everybody was busy and seemed to forget about me. I tried to sneak away, but the man that captured me came and got me and brought me back to the village. He sat me down by the fire and tried to explain to me: 'You stay here. You stay here. Don't run away.' At this time, I was starting to understand some of the language that they were speaking. Even though I tried speaking my own Mi'kmaw language, there was very little communication. The only thing that I understood was that they wanted me to stay. They weren't mean to me; they treated me like all the other children. So, I became a little comfortable in the surroundings. After a while they painted me with the same red paint that they had painted on their own bodies. I'm sure I must have looked like one of them.

And after a while I became comfortable living with them, and I felt as if I was one of their own. I played and hunted with them; I played the same kind of games that they played.

"An old woman befriended me. She fed me, and every day she would make me go down to the river with her and she would pray. I assumed it was praying. She pointed to the sky a lot, and to the water and to the land, and she made me do the same thing. It was then I remembered my own teachings of my own grandmother who would do the same thing. We would go to the river and we would pray and give thanks for all the wonderful things that we have in our life. We would give thanks for the food and the land and the water. We would give thanks for the qalipu that was an important part in our life; it was life-giving and provided shelter and transportation.

"So, after a while I became comfortable with this Beothuk woman that had befriended me and was teaching me some of their ways. I eventually became good friends with the tall man that captured me, and he talked to me and after a while I understood. He also came to understand some of the Mi'kmaw language that I spoke.

"After about two years, I was out hunting with a bunch of young people my own age; I was about eight years old, and we were up on this high hill and I looked off in the distance and I saw smoke. I wondered if this was my own people. So, when nobody was looking, I snuck away. When I got in the woods, I had no idea how far the campsite was. I kept running and running and running 'til I fell down, and I rested for a while. And I listened. Nobody was following me. After a long time, I got up and I started running again. I came to a big lake, and the smoke from the campsite was on the other side of the lake. The lake was too big for me to swim, so I knew I had to walk all around the lake. I still wasn't sure if this was my people or another family of Beothuk people that was travelling on the land.

"As I was walking around a sharp point in the lake, I was confronted by two Mi'kmaw men in a qalipu-skin gwitn. They came ashore very quickly; they must have thought that I was a Beothuk boy, but they kept talking to me in Mi'kmaq and I replied to them in Mi'kmaq. I told them who I was. I told them who my grandfather and my grandmother were, how I had been captured by the Beothuk for two years, and how I was trying to find my own people. They took me down to the water's edge and washed the red ochre from my face, my hands, and my body.

"They then took me back to their camp where the women and children were, and they fed me and we talked some more—way into the night. They told me that they would take me to my grandfather and my grandmother; they knew where they were camping.

"And I was never afraid, my whole two years, except for a few times in the beginning. I got very comfortable. I was able to understand the language that was being spoken, and I grew accustomed to covering myself in red ochre.

"When I arrived back in my own camp with my grandmother, grandfather, uncles, father, and mother, there was much joy, much dancing, and much celebration. I was a young hero because I had lived with the Beothuk people and I had escaped and come back to my own people. I was asked many questions that night in my grandfather's lodge about where I had been, what I had seen, and what it was like to live with the Beothuk people. I told them that we picked berries; we hunted for qalipu; we hunted for fish; we went down to the sea to gather shellfish, salmon, and cod fish. All those things that we had done, I had also done in the Beothuk camp. They were friendly and treated me as one of them.

"So you see, Suliewey, the man I spoke to last night was the son of the man that captured me. And he remembered me when I talked to him. The Beothuk are on the move; they are going to Pmaqtin, the Sacred Mountain, to pray. But they are on the move. They are very afraid of the white men and what they are doing to the Beothuk. There are stories all across the island that the Beothuk people are being shot on sight by the white men.

"When they went to their summer campsite to fish and to get food for the summer and for the winter, they were shot at. So that man last night was telling me to be very careful. He didn't want the rest of his group to know that we are so close, because he didn't know what they would do. They are very angry and afraid, and he told me not to come too close. But he also said he would go back and tell the story that he had seen the young man that lived with them for all those years, many years ago.

"When I lived with the Beothuk people, they called me a funny name that I didn't understand. To my own people, I was known as the lpa'tu'jij with the silver hair. You see, I had a small streak of silver hair, just as you have. When they see you, and they see that silver hair on your head, they will know that you are related to me and they will remember, because there's still people in that village that remember that time.

"So it's not that I'm afraid of them. I just don't want the white men to find a way to get to them. I don't want the white men to track us and find where they're heading. You see, Suliewey, the Beothuk are our people too. Even though we speak a different language, they are our people and we will try everything we can to protect them—always. They are being hunted, and eventually, if the slaughter continues of their people, there will be no one left. So when we get back to our village, we will speak to the Elders about our journey and about what we saw.

"But we, too, have to go to the mountain to pray and to leave gifts of wild tobacco for the Wuklatmu'jk—the little people—to give thanks for all that we have. And we must pray for good hunting, so that when we come back to the grandmothers and the village, we will bring back much food. Now we must sleep, Lpa'tu'jij. In the morning we will continue our journey."

Chapter 5 — **TRAVEL TO U'NAMA'KIK**

I t was early fall when sixteen-year-old Suliewey, later known as Sylvester Joe, had set off on his journey from Miawpukek to Nujio'qonikllek—the area known to the Europeans as St. George's Bay. His grandfather had paddled him across the river in a gwitn; he then walked overland for four weeks with only the clothes on his back, a small amount of food, and the new pair of moccasins that his grandmother had made for him. On his arrival at the village of Flat Bay, Suliewey met others from Miawpukek who had moved there, and was welcomed into their home to spend the night. The next morning, he headed to the shore to see if there was a ship going to U'nama'kik; that is where he wanted to go. He wanted to see U'nama'kik because he had heard so much about it from his family, his grandfather, and other relatives who often spoke of the place. He was curious and wanted to see U'nama'kik for himself and see what it was all about.

When he arrived at the shore, there was a schooner getting ready to sail across to U'nama'kik. Suliewey walked up to the captain and in broken English he said, "I'm looking for a ride to Nova Scotia in your schooner; can I go with you? I am willing to work."

The captain looked him up and down, saw his ragged clothes and long hair, and said to Suliewey, "Get lost you savage. I don't want you on my boat. Get out of here." Suliewey looked at the captain for a long time and then turned and walked away. He did not go very far, just around the bend in the road, and then walked off through the woods. There he made a small fire and some tea and waited. It was early afternoon, a warm sunny day, and Suliewey lay by the fire and slept. Every so often he would wake up and check to see if the captain was still around, and he was.

Finally, it was dark and he heard the captain, the mate, and other members of the crew walking down the road. From what Suliewey could understand, they were going to the local tavern down the road to drink some beer before sailing to Nova Scotia. When they passed where Suliewey was hiding in the bush, he waited until they went by, then he went down to the shore to board the schooner. His plan was to stow away on the schooner and go to U'nama'kik. He looked around on the ship and then finally lifted a small hatch that led down to the hold of the ship. He climbed down the ladder and found a small place behind some barrels. He covered himself in a piece of sail canvas and went to sleep.

Sometime during the night, Suliewey was awakened by loud noises, as though people were arguing and fighting on deck. The captain and his crew had come back aboard the boat while Suliewey was asleep, and they were arguing. The crew didn't want to go to Nova Scotia that night; they wanted to wait until morning. The captain was determined that he was going that night and in a loud voice said to his mate and crew, "Untie the damn schooner! We are leaving tonight!" Suliewey was terrified that they would come down into the hold and find him. Suliewey lay very quietly, listening to the noises of the schooner getting underway, then he pulled the tarp over his shoulders and went to sleep.

When he awoke the next time, the schooner was a fair way out to sea and was bobbing, weaving, and pounding in the waves. For the first time in his life Suliewey felt terribly ill; he was seasick but knew nothing about seasickness. He had never been on a boat before and did not know why he felt ill. As he lay there, he wondered if it was something that he had eaten, or if it was something from where he was sleeping in the ship that was making him sick.

Suliewey got up from behind the barrels; as he did so, he fell over a barrel and made a loud noise. He heard voices on deck and the captain saying to the crew, "Go below to see what the noise is and what is happening down there." Suliewey sneaked back behind the barrels again. There was a light shining through the opening to the hold and the mate came down holding a lantern with a lit candle in it, shining it around to see what the noise was. Suliewey tried to be as quiet as he could and not make any noise. One of the other men went around the barrels and looked over them, but he could not see what had caused the noise. He swore to himself and said, "It must be those damn rats again." He then climbed up the ladder to the deck. With relief, Suliewey tried to go back to sleep again.

All night long and into the next day the schooner pounded along in the waves and wind; finally, late into the evening the schooner arrived in U'nama'kik and anchored in the harbour. While the captain and crew were talking,

Suliewey slipped over the side of the ship and swam to shore. He waited on shore for the captain and his crew to come ashore; when the captain stepped down onto land, the first person he saw was Suliewey, who was soaked to the skin. The captain said to Suliewey, "Where did you come from, you savage? How did you get here?"

Suliewey's response was, "I just wanted to make sure that you arrived safe and sound in U'nama'kik, sir, and was here to meet and greet you." And with that, he walked away. He could hear the captain saying something, but he did not stay around to find out what it was. He then walked from the harbour up to a small village called Membertou, along the Membertou River. Suliewey was surprised with the conditions of the homes that were there.

He spoke to people that were just like himself; their clothes were like his, and he was glad to find someone that spoke a language that he could understand. Suliewey learned from the Mi'kmaq in U'nama'kik, and told stories of life in Newfoundland. For a while he roamed around Nova Scotia, as the white people called it, going from village to village learning about his own history and culture and speaking the language. Suliewey became friends with several Mi'kmaw Elder trappers and they invited him to go trapping with them. Suliewey went trapping for beaver, lynx, fox, and other animals that were available.

After some time, Suliewey decided it was time to go back home and take his place among the village and the people of Miawpukek. Suliewey went to the dock and arranged passage aboard a schooner to Mikl'n—a French island off the coast of Newfoundland, which the French called Miquelon. The captain was welcoming and invited him to come along with them if he was willing to work alongside the rest of the Mi'kmaq that were travelling to Mikl'n.

Chapter 6 → **SULIEWEY'S RETURN VIA MIQUELON**

When Suliewey got to Mikl'n from U'nama'kik on the schooner, he was surprised to see so many birchbark wikuoms on the beach; how welcomed he felt, not only by his own people, but by the French people of Mikl'n who welcomed him like a long-lost brother. He found his way down to the beach where the Mi'kmaw families were camped. He saw that they had ocean-going gwitns with them and he thought, *"This is my way home, back to Miawpukek."* He would get a ride with a Mi'kmaw family that was going back to Taqamkuk. So he stayed in Mikl'n for a week or so. Then he saw a family making ready to travel back to Taqamkuk on a clear, moonlit night. The water was so calm it looked like glass. Suliewey knew this was the time for him to return home to Miawpukek. He sat in the bow of the gwitn with the Mi'kmaw man, his family, all their belongings, their food, and their covering for the night. When they left, they headed for a place called Pass Island. When they got to Pass Island, they knew that the rest of the way to Miawpukek was fairly calm and good. So they spent the day on Pass Island, just sitting around and talking. Suliewey was so pleased to be back, close to his own land again and talking to people in the language that he knew best; the ancient Mi'kmaw language had been spoken in Ktaqamkuk for uncounted years. Suliewey was happy that he was going home.

Then next day when the tide was rising and there was no wind on the water, they left Pass Island and headed into Miawpukek. It took them another day. They spent the next night in a small cove on Gaultois Island; again, they talked way into the night, drinking tea. The next day, at the break of dawn when the sun was just coming over the hills, they put their gwitn in the water again and left to paddle the last few miles into Miawpukek. When they got into Lu'tik—now called Roti Bay—the wind had come up, so they had to stay in the cove again for one more night. Miawpukek was just around the head of Qa'qawejwe'katik—Crow Head—and Suliewey was so anxious to get home to see his family again and to start living with them and helping out where he could.

When he finally arrived, all the village came to welcome him home. His grandmother hugged him and said "Pjilasi! Keselul, Lpa'tu'jij." The women prepared a feast, and the Elders prepared a Sweat Lodge. After the Sweat Lodge, they feasted, and Suliewey sat in the Chief's wikuom that night with the Elders so they could hear his stories about the villages he had seen, the people he had spoken with, and the things he had learned about himself—his own strengths and weaknesses.

Everybody wanted to hear the news about U'nama'kik. Suliewey became a storyteller; night after night he would sit in someone's wikuom and tell stories of what was happening in the rest of the Mi'kmaw nation. He told stories about what was happening in the rest of the mainland. He had learned many stories about the Kji' Saqamaw, the Grand Chief, including why the Grand Chief had decided he would accept Christianity and become the first Mi'kmaw to be Christian, in Louisburg in 1610. He told that story many, many times over. But he also heard many stories of how the Beothuk people were being treated in the north. He remembered his grandfather's stories of being a captive all those years ago. As he talked more and more every night, he started to remember some of those words that he had long forgotten. He remembered some of the language that his grandfather had taught him, and he vowed that someday he would go and find any Beothuk people that were out there and try to make friends. He knew that his grandfather had been accepted because of the silver streak in his hair. Suliewey also had a silver streak in his hair, and he knew that if he ever came across the Beothuk people, he would be recognized by the silver streak.

Suliewey started trapping again with his grandfather, his uncles, and his father. They travelled inland from Miawpukek up to Cold Springs Pond, into T'maqanap-skwe'katik, and on into Beothuk territory to trap animals that were available. In their travels they found the remains of Beothuk camps. They travelled further west, and one evening just before the sun went down, Suliewey was sitting on top of a high hill. Off in the distance he could see a little bit of smoke coming up from among the trees along the lake. As he sat by the little fire that night trying to stay warm, he wondered what would happen if he met with Beothuk people. But he knew their hunting area was too far south, and the Beothuk had been driven further north by the white men.

After trapping all winter Suliewey decided in the spring that he would take his furs to a place called Hermitage. In Hermitage there was a merchant that bought furs—

beaver, otter, and other furs that were brought to him. While Suliewey was there, the merchant mentioned that there was a white man by the name of Cormack, in the city of St. John's, looking for a Mi'kmaw guide to lead him across the island of Newfoundland while he looked for the Beothuk people. The merchant asked Suliewey if he would he be interested in doing that, since it was along part of his trapline just east of there. The merchant was sure that this man would pay good money. Suliewey agreed to take on the job of guiding Cormack across the interior of Ktaqamkuk. But as he walked out the door, he thought to himself, *"I don't want to guide a white man to where the Beothuk people are."*

When he arrived home, Suliewey spoke with his grandfather and the other Elders and told them about this strange request. His grandfather listened to Suliewey talk about this journey that this man was taking across Ktaqamkuk to look for Beothuk people. Grandfather said to Suliewey, "If you do this you cannot show this man where the Beothuk people live. Look at what they have done so far. Look how many people have been killed. If you show him where the remainder of the Beothuk people live, you will be as responsible for their death as the Europeans that have gone in to slaughter them. I want you to think long and clear before you do this." Suliewey said he would.

That night, the village Elders built a Sweat Lodge and invited Suliewey to come into it, saying they would pray for him and for his strength and health. In the Sweat Lodge the village Elders prayed that the Beothuk people would be spared and that Cormack wouldn't find them. They also encouraged Suliewey to be honest and show the man the way across the island, but not to show him where the Beothuk lived. Suliewey, in his own prayers, asked for the strength and wisdom that he would need to be honest with this man and to show him the way across Ktaqamkuk.

When the Sweat Lodge ceremony was over, his grandmother met him at the door with a bundle containing new moccasins, bread that she had made that day, a shirt, and other things that he would need on his journey. She said, "May the Great Spirit be with you and guide you and bring you safely back to us."

Chapter 7 → COMING TO ST. JOHN'S

Suliewey left Miawpukek just as the sun was coming over the eastern hills. When he reached the top of the hill looking back at the village, he could see the houses of his grandfather, his parents, and his brothers and sisters, and wondered when he would return to the village again. His grandfather stood outside and watched Suliewey walk up the road and over the hill, with what looked like the weight of the world on his back in such a small bundle for someone travelling so far. He whispered a prayer of thankfulness that his grandson would be safe, strong, and wise.

When he arrived in St. John's, Suliewey was surprised at how it smelled and looked, and how much noise there was. He found his way through the city down to the docks and asked for the company called Newman's. He was directed to a wharf and told to ask the merchant for Newman Company in a big building. When he got to the door of Newman Company and walked in, he felt like he was trapped; he was afraid to close the door. There was a man sitting behind the desk who looked at him and said, "Close the bloody door! You are letting in the cold!"

Suliewey closed the door and walked very quietly up to the desk. He said, "My name is Suliewey, I come from Miawpukek. I was sent by a merchant from Hermitage to ask for a man by the name of Cormack, who wishes me to guide him across the island of Newfoundland."

The man said, "We have been waiting for you. We had a letter from Newman's in Hermitage saying that you were on the way." Suliewey was then told, "Come back to this office at six o'clock and Mr. Cormack will meet you here. He will then discuss his journey and the provisions that he will need you to have and the kind of accommodations that he will have for you." The man then ushered Suliewey out the door.

After Suliewey left Newman Company, he found his

way down to the dock and a place that seemed to be out of everyone's way. He then settled down and thought about his trip from Miawpukek to St. John's. He thought about all the animals that he saw on his journey. He thought about the warm sunny days, and at times throughout the afternoon he found himself wondering what he was doing in a place like this. People that worked on the docks looked at him in a way that made him feel like he was doing something wrong; even a dog came by and snarled at him. Eventually Suliewey realized that it was getting close to the time that he was to meet this fellow, Cormack. He made his way back from the dock to the office of Cormack at Newman's. When he arrived at Newman Company and walked in, the man behind the desk told him, "We received a message from Mr. Cormack saying that he will not be here today, but you can come back tomorrow and he will see you then."

Suliewey left, not sure what to do. He had left a small bundle in a wooded area just outside of town. Even though it was early evening, he decided that he would go back to the place where the bundle was; at least there he could make a fire, have tea, and there was a blanket to keep him warm during the night. After walking for about an hour and a half, Suliewey came to the small area of woods where he had left the bundle. He was glad to be comfortable; after he made fire and had tea, he lay down by the fire and fell asleep.

Throughout the night Suliewey dreamed of Miawpukek and all the beautiful people there: his grandmother, grandfather, parents, brothers, and sisters. The village itself was such a peaceful place. Suliewey longed to be back there again; he woke from sleep more than once, wondering why he was in a place like this. Then he remembered his grandfather's advice: "If you meet this man, please don't let him visit the Beothuk people because we don't know what his intentions are." Suliewey then went back to sleep.

Chapter 8 — **THE TEST OF FIDELITY**

T he next day, Suliewey returned to St. John's, where he finally met up with Cormack. Cormack said to Suliewey, "From now on you will be my Indian."

Suliewey responded, "My name is not My Indian. My church name is Sylvester."

Cormack said, "I will call you Sylvester, but neverthe-less, you're my Indian."

Again, Suliewey said, "I'm not your Indian."

Cormack replied, "You're my Indian."

"Yes, nei'n Aqalasie'w," Suliewey finally said.

"What does that mean?"

Suliewey turned away and smiled. "Oh, that means you're the boss."

William Cormack sat down with Suliewey and told him that he would take him on a walk of approximately one hundred and fifty miles, from Holyrood to Placentia. The reason he wanted to do that, he told Suliewey, was to test his fidelity. Suliewey had no idea what fidelity meant, so he asked Cormack, "What do you mean by fidelity?"

"I mean I want to test your honesty and your strength and your courage, to make sure you can take me across the island of Newfoundland and you can find the Beothuk people. This will be a test of your character, Sylvester."

Suliewey just looked at Cormack. "I've walked from Miawpukek to St. John's to meet you and now you're going to make me walk one hundred and fifty miles to test my strength?" He turned and walked away.

Cormack said to him, "Come back! We need to discuss this some more."

Suliewey turned and looked at Cormack and said, "I need to go away, and I will come back tomorrow and let you know if I'm strong enough to do that."

Suliewey returned the next day and told Cormack that he would walk with him from Holyrood to Placentia and back to St. John's. He told Cormack, "If you don't like how I work and walk, and how I do my fair share and help you to go safely, then I will go back to Miawpukek and you can find someone else. I promise you this."

They gathered the things they were going to take on their journey across the Avalon for Cormack's test of Suliewey's strength. It was like he was testing an animal. Suliewey watched Cormack pack a bundle that had very little in it; of the journey supplies they had to take, Suliewey had to carry everything. He watched Cormack pack his own bundle with extra warm clothes; Suliewey only had the clothes that he wore on his back and a brand-new pair of skin boots in his bundle that his grandmother had made for him before he left home.

Cormack looked at Suliewey and said, "You are my Indian. Here's what I want you to do. For the next few days, we will gather the equipment we will need to take with us on this trip. It is now July and we should be back in St. John's in early August. Along the way, we should find fish that we can eat. There will be some berries that we can eat. Also, on the trail from Holyrood to Placentia, there will be many qalipu. And in some places, we may even find salmon. Not just trout, but salmon."

Suliewey thought of what Cormack had said: *"You are my Indian."* He felt it necessary to correct Cormack. "You can own a gun. You can own a knife. You can own a dog.

But you can't own a person. I'm not your Indian. You do not own me," he said.

Then they left on their journey and walked over one hundred miles just to test Suliewey's skills and strength. Even though Cormack walked with him, the bundle that he carried wasn't as heavy or as big as the one Suliewey was expected to carry. When they camped that night, it was Suliewey who went and got the firewood, made a fire, got water for the tea, got water for the supper, and got the camp ready for Cormack. He went and picked the boughs and made Cormack as comfortable as he possibly could.

While Cormack wrote in his journal and drew pictures that Suliewey didn't understand, Suliewey chipped on his own walking stick. He had a stick that he carried with him all day, and he put symbols on his stick to mark the days, the number of animals he had seen along the way, and whether they were beaver, qalipu, or otter— all the animals that they saw. One day Cormack asked him, "Why are you putting those marks on your walking stick?"

Suliewey said, "This is my stick to tell the journey of where I'm going and what I'm doing." He said, "You write in your funny book and I mark on my stick. It's the same thing. You call your book your journal. I simply call mine my stick and it marks my journey."

Upon their return from Placentia, Cormack decided

that he would go back to St. John's by way of Trinity and Conception Bay. Cormack simply said to Suliewey, "You're a good Indian. Now we will make the big journey. We will go up the coast in a schooner, and then we will make our way across the island."

In the back of Suliewey's mind, he knew that with him, Cormack was never going to find the Beothuk people. He knew that at all costs, he was to keep Cormack as far south as he possibly could.

SYLVESTER'S TALE

Chapter 9 — THE JOURNEY BEGINS

At the end of our one hundred and fifty mile walk to Plisantek—what he called Placentia—I thought that it might be clear to Cormack that I was honest and honourable and that I had done what he wanted. Cormack looked at me and said, "I'll meet you in a couple of weeks at Newman's." He did not invite me to his house. So I went back to my campsite from earlier in July when I first reached St. John's.

Two weeks later when I met him in St. John's, Cormack came to me and informed me that we must prepare to leave, as it was now the end of August. As Cormack turned away, he asked if I was okay with that, but he kept on walking without waiting for my answer. I spoke anyway, and said, "Maybe we should have left earlier. We wasted time walking across Placentia to see if I was capable of guiding you across the island."

Cormack turned and said, "Did you say something, Indian?"

"Yes. I said, maybe we should have gone much earlier to Random Sound. Leaving this late we may run into bad weather and be forced to go south to avoid it."

"No," said Cormack, "We go now at the end of this month. I want to find the Beothuk campsite sooner rather than later."

I felt that Cormack hoped he would find their camp early on in our journey and would not have to go all the way across the island.

By the next morning, Cormack was ready. "Here's the equipment that we are going to need," he said, thinking I was going to correct him.

I said, "I have my own gun, my own axe, my own blanket, my own bundle, which I used to walk the two hundred miles to get here. Whatever food we need we can bring with us, and along the way we can shoot wild geese, shoot ducks, catch fish, and we can even shoot a nice fat qalipu. Now we're ready, Aqalasie'w."

We left St. John's by schooner at the end of August and headed for Trinity Bay to start our journey across the island, which would take many days of hard walking.

On our way up the east coast, I spent most of my time standing at the rail of the ship watching the coastline go by. I felt a deep sense of loneliness, missing my family back in Miawpukek and remembering the last conversation I had with my Elders. Was I taking this man to find the Beothuk? And if by chance we came across their campsite, would Cormack shoot to defend us if attacked? I am sure Cormack would be called a hero and me, the lone Indian, would take the blame for such a deed. The white man's laws would not believe me and my side of the story. During this time, Cormack never spoke to me or acknowledged me in any way. As the coastline slipped past the ship, Cormack would sketch pictures in his book and write his words.

On August 30 we sailed past Conception Bay and on past Baccalieu Island. On this island, like many other islands around Newfoundland, eggers—men who collected seabird eggs—would show up in small boats and schooners. The men would carry off boatloads of newly laid eggs and take all the eggs they could find, not thinking about the survival of those birds. I thought back to being on the land with my grandfather. Many times, we would gather the eggs from seagulls and other birds like geese and ducks. We never took more than one or two eggs from each nest, leaving the rest as we have done for hundreds of years, and our food source remained healthy.

On August 31 we arrived in Bonaventure, a small fishing harbour on the west side of Trinity Bay. It was here in this small harbour that Cormack asked for information about the interior, and engaged a local fisherman with a small skiff to take us to Random Sound. As in other places in Newfoundland, no one had any information; they did not normally go very far from the salt water for firewood and boat-building materials for their fishing boats. Some of the people in the harbour said there was fear that the savages would kill them and steal their women and children. Cormack pointed to me and said, "I am travelling with my Indian. He will protect me. Have you seen any of the Beothuk that you are so afraid of?"

"No," was the response. "We only hear stories about such things."

I heard a low voice say, "Shoot the savages on sight, sir! And be careful of the savage with you. He might slit your throat while you sleep."

Cormack did not respond to that remark and just walked away.

Cormack decided that we would go inland as far as the smaller boat could go, avoiding the long walk overland. The overland hike would take at least six or seven days over rough land and high, wooded hills. The boat would take us to the west part of Random Sound.

On September 3 we left Bonaventure aboard the skiff with two local fishermen; we expected to travel to the southwest for at least six miles. As we drew closer to the shallow end of the sound, at Random Bar, we saw evidence of the white man, who came to this area to peel the bark from the balsam fir. They used it on their flakes to cover their cod while it was drying. I have seen my own people peel balsam fir, but for a different purpose. In the springtime, when the sap started to run, large pieces of bark were taken from the trees and we would lay the bark on the ground with rocks on top to keep them flat. When dried, the bark could be used to cover our tilts or wikuoms in the summertime as a temporary shelter. Over the summer, the tops of these trees would turn red and the wood would be cut in late fall for firewood.

Along the way I noticed that there was an abundance of birchbark, which we used for building ocean-going gwitns. I pointed this out to Cormack, and said, "Our people gather this bark to build our gwitns. The Beothuk use this same bark for their gwitns, and they travel long distances offshore to Funk Island and other islands to gather eggs, which, like our own people, is a very important part of their winter food supply."

Our boat lay dry on the bar all night, and Cormack insisted that we sleep in the small boat that night. I was thinking, *"Why not set up camp on shore where we could have a fire and make tea and hot food?"* I think maybe Cormack was afraid to leave the safety of his white friends and that he might be having second thoughts about the long, hard journey ahead.

After spending the night with Cormack and his friends in a small boat, sleeping on bare boards, I longed to be in the woods with a fire. But Cormack was afraid that there might be wolves or even wild Indians, as he called the Beothuk. I knew that there were no wolves on this coast and I also knew there were no "wild Indians". When I promised Cormack I would guide him on this journey, I was obligated to stay with him and not voice my opinion that we were safe enough on this coast. I knew before I left home that my brothers and sisters of the Beothuk people were nowhere near this coast at this time of year.

When we left the coast in the morning, I knew it would be hard going for Cormack, and even for myself, even though I had crossed this land many times in my life. Most of the supplies that Cormack wanted to take with him were left to me; I wondered what he would be carrying. When we repacked our bundles that morning, I watched very closely to see what Cormack was putting in his: a few of his personal belongings, a small amount of food, and a lot of shot for his gun. Most of the provisions were left to me to put in my bundle. I pointed out to Cormack the route we would use to move westward. I also asked him if we would need to collect medicines along the way.

He replied to me in a rough voice, "No. Absolutely not. I have all the medicines I need. And I probably know more about the plants that we will be seeing than you do. I have been taught by the best teachers that we have."

"Yes, Aqalasie'w."

On September 5, 1822, we thanked the party that brought Cormack and me this far. The party then left us and returned to Bonaventure. I was surprised that Cormack kept firing shots in the air until he could no longer hear the return of shots from the boat.

After many hours of travel, the weight of our bundles seemed to get heavier. We had only travelled maybe two or three miles at best. While Cormack was resting, I climbed a tall tree to look westward to find the best routes for us to travel. What I saw to the west about fifteen or twenty miles ahead looked like nothing but very dense bush. I knew that beyond twenty miles, we would find open country with lots of bog and swamp. I deliberately didn't tell Cormack of the conditions that we were facing in the next little while.

After Cormack had rested, we decided to travel further northwest until just before sunset. At times I looked back at Cormack to see if he was doing okay. Sometimes he would stop to write in his funny-looking book. I would stand or sit patiently, waiting for him to catch up. I often wondered what he was writing about.

The journey we were taking was not going to be an easy one. It was rough walking through the bog with the young growth and the scrub growth, and I knew that we would not make good time. I knew that Cormack was also having a hard time, even though his bundle was not as big as mine. But he kept up. It was a long way to go from Random Sound to the west coast of Newfoundland.

Oftentimes, I would leave to find medicines that I needed for the day, all the while looking for smoke from other campsites. I carried bear fat in my bundle that I would rub onto my feet if they were sore, while my skin boots were drying. Not once did Cormack ask about the kind of medicines that I was using for my feet or for my stomach. I wondered at times if Cormack was more interested in searching for the many resources of Ktaqamkuk that could make his colony a rich place for the British, than he was in searching for the Beothuk.

At our first night's camp, after five or six miles of slogging through heavy brush, timber, and bog, I was still expected to do additional work. Cormack kept referring to me as 'My Indian,' and each time he did that, I would simply say, "Yes, Aqalasie'w."

Once in a while, Cormack would look at me and ask me what 'aqalasie'w' meant. I would tell him, "I'm just saying you're the boss." Not once did Cormack ask me for the English translation; I didn't intend to give him one.

For the first night's camp we picked a dry area where I could find moss and some balsam fir boughs to make a comfortable bed for Cormack. I shot a partridge and I cooked it for our supper while Cormack wrote in his book. After I did all the camp chores, and when supper was over, I put more wood on the fire. Then I sat down next to the fire with my pipe and carved the events of the day's journey on my stick, including the partridge that I had shot for supper. From time to time, I would put a symbol meaning Cormack on my stick.

The next morning, we picked up our bundles and left our campsite to continue our journey. Now I felt more at home. We travelled in a northwesterly direction, knowing that there was no road or trail to follow. The centre of the island was nearly west from us.

After hours of tough going through thick woods with the heavy packs, again we had only travelled a short distance from the coast. The way west, I knew, would be covered with heavy forest. Just before sunset we made camp. I walked a short distance to a small stream to get water for tea. It was here I first saw tracks—moccasin tracks, which did not look like Mi'kmaw tracks. I chose not to tell Cormack what I had seen. Back at our camp, I rolled up in my blanket and fell asleep with the sweet smell of the land and the tall trees around us. I fell asleep thinking, *"I'm home."*

The next morning when I woke up my right eye was red and swollen. Cormack tried looking to see if there was something in my eye, but he said he didn't see anything. We packed our bundles and started walking. During the day we passed through lush forest and great areas of bogland. All the while I searched for a special plant that my grandmother had taught me about. The plant had a hollow filled with liquid that I could use to cure the swelling and soreness. After walking for a short while, I spotted the plant.

Cormack watched me take the plant and check it for clear water, which I then poured in my eye. He said, "Crazy Indian" and walked away. As we walked, I pointed out to Cormack the medicine I saw: yellow root, beaver root, tips of the balsam fir trees, alder leaves, the leaves of the blueberry plant, and many more. Cormack's only comment was, "All hogwash, Indian. It's just plants. We have doctors now that make great medicine to cure anything."

"No doctor here, Aqalasie'w. Only me."

Cormack snorted something and walked away.

Later that day just before we made camp, Cormack walked over to me and without asking grabbed my face and looked at my eye. The swelling and soreness were gone. Cormack just turned and walked away.

Chapter 10 → CAMPING FOR THE NIGHT

When we stopped for the night, about an hour before dark, I was surprised to have Cormack help me set up the camp. I knew he had not been sleeping well.

"You don't mark on your book tonight," I said. "Let's make the camp comfortable tonight."

We gathered small balsam fir boughs and laid them down in a way that resembled the feathers on a duck. When our boughs were laid out, they were about four or five inches deep. Then we gathered enough wood to keep a fire going all night. After sticking poles in the ground, I spread out my bundle, and hung it over the poles just in case it rained. After the fire was going the smoke kept the swarming flies away. I walked a short distance and found a nice rabbit run; there I set a snare thinking that we could have rabbit for lunch the following day. To my surprise, when I was almost back to the camp, I heard the cry of a rabbit in the snare. *"Supper,"* I thought.

After a supper of roasted rabbit, it was time to crawl into our blankets to rest and sleep after a long, hard day of slogging through dense woods with swarms of black flies attacking us. As we lay on the sweet-smelling boughs, for a few moments I watched the smoke drift up through the trees. When I awoke it was just on the edge of another day. How glorious it was to be in this special place. My heart was happy.

After another hard day of walking, just before sunset we settled in some thick forest and built a camp. While Cormack sat on a rock and wrote in his book, I gathered wood and made a fire. The weather was good; we didn't expect rain, so we had no need of a shelter. That night while the fire was burning bright, I went to the woods and collected spruce boughs to put on the ground so that we could have a comfortable sleep with our feet to the fire and our skin boots would dry. Again, Cormack called me 'his Indian.' I was bothered by this. My pride kept telling me that I was nobody's Indian. This man was out in the wilds of Newfoundland with only me to protect him from any danger that might be out there, yet he continued to insult me by referring to me as 'his.'

At times I thought of referring to Cormack as 'my clumsy aqalasie'w,' but because of the promise I had made to the Elders of my village, I chose at that time not to make my thoughts known to this man. I wrapped myself in my blanket and went to sleep.

I woke early in the morning, and while Cormack rested on the bed of boughs, I climbed up a small hill to look ahead for any signs of smoke that would mean there were some of my people nearby. Cormack was still sleeping on my return to our campsite. I made a fire, then went to a small stream to wash and to pray to the four directions that we might have a safe journey again today. While I sat by the stream, I thought of the things that my Elders told me. I prayed to the great-grandmothers that they would always protect us on our journey, and most of all to look after our Beothuk brothers and sisters.

Chapter 11 → **SWEAT LODGE HEALING**

During our travels Cormack and I ran into wet weather, and Cormack developed a cough. I watched Cormack get sicker by the day. After a few days, I knew it was time. When camp was made that evening, I said to Cormack, "I think I need to make you strong medicine."

After a long bout of coughing Cormack replied, "I have good medicine with me, I don't need your savage kind of medicine."

Despite Cormack's opposition, early the next morning

I rose from the campsite and went to collect the seven medicines that I needed to help Cormack get well. I collected alder bark, tips of balsam fir, Indian tea leaves, cherry bark, blueberry leaves, mint berry leaves, and ground juniper. I had been taught that these seven medicines represent the seven virtues of life. The alder bark was used for headaches, aches and pains, and soreness. Cherry bark was used for coughs; ground juniper for kidney problems and back pain; blueberry leaves and Indian tea to take away toxins; tips of balsam fir to help build strength; and mint berry leaves to add a soothing scent and taste.

When I arrived back at camp, Cormack once again displayed arrogance against the medicines that I had collected. He said to me, "We should rest here for the day."

It was fortunate that our campsite was situated near a large bed of alders. Despite Cormack's arrogance, I decided to build a Sweat Lodge to help cure Cormack of his illness. While Cormack lay in the lean-to, coughing, I got twelve long alder saplings and made a frame. I then went and collected birchbark to cover the lodge that I had made for myself and Cormack. I collected moss to cover the entire structure and maintain the heat from the grandfathers— as we call the stones—that would be placed inside.

I made a birchbark container and filled it with water, then put the seven medicines in it. I then hung the bark container over the fire to heat; while it did so, I placed seven large grandfathers on the fire. As I did all this Cormack looked on in amazement, but never said a word. When the grandfathers were red hot, I used a forked stick to place them inside the small lodge. I then invited Cormack to come inside the lodge with me. Reluctantly Cormack came into the lodge. Once we were both inside, I closed the small door, which made the lodge very dark. I put an offering of tobacco on the hot grandfather stones and said, "Now we will pray for your good health," as I splashed water from the seven medicines onto the stones.

For me the Sweat Lodge was cleansing and energy-giving, but Cormack gave no acknowledgement of how he felt, or if it did him any good. He muttered something under his breath, but I didn't understand. It was not spoken of again.

The following morning, we left our camp and continued our journey west. I watched what Cormack was putting in his bundle. Once again, it was very little; most of our supplies I carried on my back in my bundle. With no open ground for miles, I knew it was going to be hard going for Cormack. I tried to find the easiest way forward, despite the heavy woods. There were many black flies and it was very hot under the trees. We only made it five or six miles that day.

It was hot and suffocating in the woods, and there

were many holes and things that can cripple a man if he was not careful of where he walked. Throughout the day many times I said to Cormack, "You follow my footsteps and you will be okay, for I know how to walk on the land."

Cormack looked at me and said, "I know what I'm doing, Indian. I don't need you to tell me how to walk on the land. All you need to do is show me where to find the red man."

Chapter 12 → BEAR FAT, MEDICINE AND SAVAGES

We continued to travel westward through heavy woods and dense undergrowth. At times we would climb a high hill that rose out of the woods. From this viewpoint we could see the westerly path ahead; it looked like we were on a steady rise from Random Sound.

For the next two or three days we struggled at a rate of seven or eight miles a day. As we progressed we found pieces of higher land where we could see the country ahead of us, and all we could see was wooded areas. Underneath the wooded areas was thick moss. We walked over the moss because it helped to protect our feet. At one point we sat on a high rock, and I tried to explain to Cormack about my people.

I took bear fat from my bundle to rub on my feet. Cormack wanted to know what I was using and why I was putting it on my feet. I explained to him that it was bear fat and it protects my feet, keeping them from getting sore and tender.

Cormack looked at me and laughed. "We have well-trained doctors who know all about how to take care of people. I have lots of medicines with me to cure anything that may be hurting me. So, my Indian. You use your bear fat and I will use the medicine that the good doctor gave me before I left St. John's."

Looking up at Cormack, I asked, "You accepted my Sweat Lodge medicines, but you don't accept my bear fat medicine?"

"It's uncivilized, Indian," he replied.

As we started on our journey again that day, we walked up to a high hill and we could see the beauty of the trees and the land, and the many things that we had to be thankful for. I asked Cormack, "Do you know that this beauty that we walk on is a form of medicine?"

He just looked at me and rolled his eyes and said, "It's just land." Then Cormack asked me, "Do you have a Bible?"

I replied, "Yes, I do. We are walking on my Bible every day." There was no reply from him for several minutes.

Then Cormack asked, "What do you mean, we are walking on your Bible?"

"This land is Mother Earth. It provides nourishment to my body, my heart, and my spirit. It provides everything I need to survive on this land. It teaches me to be strong, it teaches me to be respectful, and it teaches me to be humble. This land is not mine or yours. It belongs to all the living creatures; it belongs to all of us. And we are all responsible for this land that we walk on. So you see, this is my Bible," I explained to Cormack. "What does your Bible teach you?"

Cormack just looked at me for a long period of time and then said harshly, "We have a long way to go."

Neither of us spoke as we continued our journey; both of us were deep in thought. As we walked, we were slowly but surely moving to higher ground. We saw many boulders and outcroppings of granite. Cormack became very interested in the soil on the rocks. At times he would chip pieces off the granite, and he would sit and observe the granite and he would write in his funny little book. I tried to explain to Cormack that these faces of granite outcroppings and boulders hold a special meaning and spiritual meaning for our people. "What's so special about rocks and boulders?" he said. "It's just rocks. Just solid rocks."

I said, "Remember, I told you we are walking on my Bible. A piece of granite is a page from my Bible for me to remember this spot and where I came from."

"Such nonsense," Cormack said again. "I say to you, Indian, it is just a rock."

Suddenly Cormack jumped up and started frantically brushing at his clothes.

"Red ants," I chuckled to myself, and walked away smiling.

As we walked along that day, and for many days after, we saw such beauty in the land around us. We crossed large bogs; sometimes those bogs surrounded a lake. We had to walk around the lakes because they blocked our journey westward. We travelled to higher ground whenever possible to avoid the many traps of dense forest, large bogs, and lakes. Many times throughout the days ahead Cormack wrote in his journal, as he told me it was called. When I asked Cormack what he was writing about, he replied, "I'm drawing pictures of the plants on the land that we walk over so there will be a record for other people to follow in our footsteps."

I said to Cormack, "I know it will happen someday, but today I pray to the Great Ones that this will not happen for many years to come. The land is sacred. It gives life to our people. I can only pray that this land will always be the same as it is today."

But I knew in my heart and soul that our brothers and sisters were being driven from their hunting and fishing grounds with the coming of the white man.

Every evening just before sunset we would stop to make camp. It was the same every day: Cormack would find a dry place to sit down, while I went to find wood and water to make fire and tea. While Cormack wrote in his journal, I found spruce boughs for us to sleep on so that we would be comfortable with our feet to the fire.

One evening after we had eaten, Cormack removed his skin boots and said that his feet were hurting. I offered him some of my bear fat for his feet, but he refused.

"I have my own medicine, Indian," was his response to me. "I don't believe in your medicines and your bear fat."

I sat by the fire and removed my own skin boots and stockings. I took my bear fat from my bundle and I rubbed it into the bottoms of my feet. Cormack looked at me and said, "Do your feet hurt?"

"No," I said. "I put bear fat on my feet every day to keep them from hurting."

That night while Cormack was comfortably asleep, I crept out of the camp and walked to a hill about a mile away to see if I could spot a fire or some other sign that there was a camp nearby. I saw nothing.

When I arrived back in camp, Cormack awakened.

"Where you been, Indian?" he asked.

"I was just checking out the area."

At noon the next day, I shot a black duck and while I roasted it over the fire, Cormack wrote in his journal. He explained, "This writing I'm doing is telling a story about our walk across Newfoundland. For anyone who wants to follow this journey, they will see a map. I have drawings and writings about our trip, and this will be a map for the people to follow."

After an hour or so we picked up our bundles and continued our westward journey. Periodically we would stop so that Cormack could write in his journal and draw pictures of the plants that we came across on our walk. That evening, just before sunset, we stopped to set up camp but we couldn't find a good place. It was wet and uneven and rocky; there was very little dry wood and the trees that we needed for boughs for a bed were few and far between.

After I got a small fire going, Cormack sat by the fire and removed his skin boots and stockings. I could see that his feet were blistered and red. I once again offered him the bear fat that I use on my feet. To my surprise, he accepted it and said, "Okay, I will try your bear fat." Cormack found a dry pair of stockings, and after he had put the bear fat on his feet, he said, "It feels good, Indian. I hope it works."

I said to him, "I have walked many miles all over this island and the bear fat has kept my feet healthy."

"We shall see, Indian."

During the night I would listen for the sound of the loons so that I would know in what direction the lakes lay. We wanted to avoid the lakes and travel over higher ground, and sometimes I could tell how far away we were from the lakes by the sound of the loons. By now, we were getting closer to well-known Beothuk campsites. During the night Cormack wanted to put the fire out just in case the "red savages" were close by.

"What is a savage?" I asked Cormack.

He replied, "You, Sylvester. You are a savage. Maybe you are not as wild as others, but nevertheless you are still a savage."

This I could not understand. I asked Cormack again, "What is a savage? What does a savage look like?"

Cormack shook his head. "I cannot explain it to you now. I will try in time."

The next day we walked and we shot a couple of partridge, which was our food for supper that evening. The provisions that we had brought with us were nearly all gone. That day as we walked through the woods it was warm and humid under the trees; mosquitoes, black flies, and sand flies were plentiful. I found some ferns at the edge of the bog and rubbed them briskly between my hands to create moisture from the leaves; I rubbed this moisture on my face and hands and any exposed flesh. I advised Cormack to do the same, but he replied, "No. I don't believe in your medicine."

That night we camped in the thick woods. We found a spot near a small stream with plenty of good wood for the fire. That night, I walked to a higher hill about half a mile from our campsite to look for any smoke from campfires. After not seeing any smoke, I came back to the campsite and lay down by the fire and slept.

Chapter 13 → MEKWAYE'KATIK – THE MIDDLE RIDGE

Early the next day we came upon a fair-sized river. I knew this river; our people were able to bring their gwitns close to where we are now many times. I pointed this out to Cormack. "Our people oftentimes came in from Bonavista Bay using this river. The river is full of fish and we need fresh fish to add to our food supply."

With our own dwindling supplies we needed to get more food. We caught ten fat trout—enough to carry with us—and after cleaning them, we cooked them over an open fire and ate our fill. Loading our packs with the rest of the trout, we left the river. We moved onward until we came to a large outcropping of rock which I knew to be part of Mekwaye'Katik. If we looked back, we could see Bonavista Bay from where we stood. In this area, qalipu, wolf, bear, fox, and marten tracks were everywhere. I pointed out to Cormack that there was much money to be made in fur trapping in this area; we might be lucky enough to see my people from Miawpukek.

Later that afternoon, I spotted footprints going in the same direction as us. I chose not to tell Cormack. I had planned that night to climb to higher ground to look for signs of smoke or fire. I hoped the tracks were from people from my own village. Cormack was getting his first view of the interior of the island and he seemed pleased to see the incredible beauty that lay before us. When we looked back in the direction we had come from, we could see many lakes and bogs that we had passed along the way. The beauty was breathtaking. But I knew on our westward trail there would be many obstacles we would have to get past to get to the west coast. I said to Cormack, "My people have crossed this land many times, but you are the first white man to ever set eyes on this beautiful land."

As we moved westward, I had a sense that we were being watched. I continually looked around for signs that there might be someone trapping in this area. I knew as we travelled further, we would come upon Lapite'spe'l, called Bay d'Espoir by the Europeans. Taking a break on a small hill overlooking the west, I pointed in the direction of Miawpukek. Cormack announced that he would call this place Mount Clarence, in honour of His Royal Highness the Duke of Clarence, who had travelled to Placentia Bay during his time in the Navy.

As we moved on, we again descended into the interior. Cormack talked about the beauty of this place and about farmland. The day before, he had talked about the possibility of cottages and livestock. I had no idea what he was talking about; to have livestock and cottages on this land made no sense.

Cormack was amazed by the crisscrossing of many qalipu trails coming from every direction. I explained to Cormack that the qalipu spend their winters in the north and come south in the spring. The trails they walk on in the bog are at least two feet deep. I also explained that there were no larger animals on this island than the bear, and that the wolves relied on meat from the qalipu as much as our people did.

"The qalipu," I explained to Cormack, "is part of our life and has provided food, clothing, shelter, and transportation for our people for thousands of years. The coming of the white man to this island will someday change all these things." I continued, "We called this island *Land Across the Big Ocean*—Ktaqamkuk—and it has been our homeland for hundreds of years."

Cormack said, "You may call this land home, but to us Europeans who have come to civilize you and your people, it is called New Found Land. That name," he said, "will be on this land forever."

I asked Cormack, "What is 'civilize'?"

He said, "All your people will live in towns and cities, have jobs, and go to church to pray and ask for forgiveness of your sins and for a better way of life."

I must have stared at Cormack for a long time because he said to me, "Is there something wrong?"

I said to him, "If I must do those things to become 'civilize', then I must leave you here. You find your own way to where you want to go. I pray to the Great Spirit every day for your health and safety. My 'job' as you call it, is to look after you and make sure you are safe in every way. I know nothing of sins that I have committed, that I must ask for forgiveness. The only forgiveness I ask for from our Great Ones is for the taking of the animals that I need to feed my family, and for the land that I walk on. I know of no better life than what I have right now, and it will continue to be a way of life for my people."

Cormack just looked at me and walked away, shaking his head. I know not if he was upset, or just didn't care.

Chapter 14 → **FOOTPRINTS ON THE TRAIL**

Early the next morning, Cormack spotted something that looked like tracks on the trail. At a glance, I saw that they were Mi'kmaw moccasin tracks, heading east. Knowing full well that Cormack didn't know the difference between Mi'kmaq or Montagnais or Beothuk moccasin tracks, I made a show of looking at the tracks and determining, for Cormack's sake, that those tracks were not Beothuk but Mi'kmaq. To further satisfy Cormack, I told him they were going away from us.

Despite the fact that we had been on Mi'kmaw territory for some time now, I felt that Beothuk people were keeping a close eye on our journey to the west. That night, I decided that whenever possible, I would go over hills or lookouts to see if I could spot the Beothuk so that I could warn them. I was sure in my own mind that we were being observed on our journey westward.

After making camp that night and having our meagre supper of fried bread and tea, I built up the fire and made Cormack comfortable. Once he was sound asleep in his blankets, I knew I could slip away and climb the nearest hill to see if I could see any sign of Beothuk people and their fire. Since it was a beautiful moonlit night, I was able to easily pick my way to the top of the hill. To my amazement, I could see many tracks of Beothuk people, as if they had been watching us make camp in the evening. It was obvious that the Beothuk were watching our westward journey, but they were no longer in sight.

This became my nightly routine: making camp near a lookout and slipping off into the darkness for signs of my Beothuk brothers and sisters. I was pleased to know they were keeping a close eye as we made our way across the land to the western coast.

Chapter 15 — SHAMING SYLVESTER

By now we were more than two moons into our journey, and Cormack was getting angry. "After all this time, we have not seen a trace of the Beothuk. Look here, my Indian! It has been five weeks since we left the east coast and we are halfway to St. George's Bay." On top of this—and what would add to his frustration—was that I wanted to convince Cormack to stop our journey and go to Miawpukek, as I feared we would be overtaken by winter before reaching the west coast.

Cormack had been—through his own lack of knowledge and preparation—suffering from the effects of the changing weather and having constantly wet feet. I merely wanted him to understand my reasoning for staying in Miawpukek during the winter; my fear was that Cormack would take ill, or worse. I feared that should anything happen to Cormack, the white man's government would place the blame on me.

Cormack persisted, offering me trinkets and promises of taking me with him to Spain or Portugal. He also tried to shame me for my concern over his well-being. He accused me of threatening to leave him alone in the country and to finish the journey alone.

"NEI'N AQALASIE'W," I said. "I promised you I would make this journey, and I keep my promise."

I had given Cormack my word. When we set out, I had made Cormack a promise that I would help him complete this journey. Cormack told me he no longer had trust in my abilities to perform the task that he had given me. Since there were no signs of the Beothuk, in his frustration he tried to make me feel inferior to him and his superior knowledge, strength, and courage.

Cormack looked at me in anger, accusing me again and again of not being up to the task. I yielded to his wish to continue; I would give Cormack what he wanted. We continued westward.

Chapter 16 → SYLVESTER DISAPPEARS

Finally, one day we saw smoke. According to Cormack's book, the date was October 11, and we had just made camp for the evening. I looked over Cormack's shoulder and saw smoke off in the distance, on the other side of the lake. I knew the camp could not be Beothuk people because it was too far south for them this time of year, and that it was likely some of my own people. But I chose not to tell this to Cormack. I wanted to warn them that Cormack was searching for the Beothuk, and that I had made a promise to my Elders to keep our Beothuk brothers and sisters safe.

Cormack was excited; he thought that we had finally found a Beothuk encampment. It was near dark and too late to make our way around the lake to their campsite; we would have to wait until morning. Cormack sat down on a rock and took out his pipe. It looked as if he was in a deep-thinking mood. After a while Cormack looked at me and said, "We go to them in the morning. If they have broken camp, we follow them."

I said to Cormack, "There was an understanding for many years between the Beothuk and the Mi'kmaq that the Beothuk were to use all the coast and flatlands for their territory, and my people would stay in the south part of the island. But since they have been driven back from their normal hunting grounds and river mouths, the Beothuk people have all but disappeared. We must approach them carefully and show them that we mean them no harm."

Cormack asked, "Are you telling me that the Micmac had a treaty with the Red Man in the sharing of territory?"

"I don't know what you mean by treaty, but many years ago our people lived together as one group on the west coast at a place near Sandy Point, in Nujioqollek, what you call St. George's Bay. The Mi'kmaq and Beothuk lived together peacefully and there was intermarriage, but all that changed when a disagreement happened over the killing of a weasel in the wrong season, and a young Beothuk boy was killed."

Not giving Cormack a chance to ask any more questions, I said to him, "You stay here and have a fire and I will go and find a nice qalipu so that we will have a gift of fresh meat and qalipu hide to present in the morning."

"No fire tonight, Indian. We don't want to alert the Beothuk that we are near," Cormack replied.

Leaving Cormack to fend for himself, I walked over a small hill, looking back to see if he was out of sight. I doubled back and headed towards the lake. I knew if I followed the big bog, I would be able to see across the lake from my high lookout.

When the darkness came, I was able to see the campfire and made my way down through the thick woods to the shore of the lake. Once on the shore, I stripped birchbark and made a birch torch that I waved back and forth, making sure that the Mi'kmaq could see my fire.

I knew that it was dark enough and far enough away from Cormack that he would not be able to see my fire. Soon I could hear paddles in the water and I was so happy to hear my language spoken for the first time since I left Miawpukek many moons ago. I was welcomed by much happiness and was invited to come to the camp of my Montagnais friend, James John, and his Mi'kmaw wife. James said to me, "We have food and my wife is in camp; she will make good food for you, my friend."

On the way across the lake, I explained to my friend about Cormack, who I had left behind for the night. I told him, "Cormack is looking for the Beothuk, but I know they are gone to their winter campsite where they will be safe."

"We will go and get Cormack in the morning, and maybe feed him for a few days. We will tell him our brothers and sisters, the Beothuk, are nowhere around here," James said.

Before the sun was up my friend took me back over to the other side of the lake and returned to his camp. I found a nice mossy place in the woods, and after all the food we had eaten during the night, telling stories, and singing Mi'kmaw songs, I drifted off to sleep.

The loud boom of a musket woke me. For a while I was confused, but as soon as I became fully awake, I realized Cormack was close by, and judging by the sun it was well after noon time. Soon I heard a return boom from across the lake and I knew I must go and meet the angry aqalasie'w. I knew he was going to be mad.

"Indian, I thought you got lost, or deserted me, or got captured by the hostile Red Indians," Cormack said when he saw me.

"Nei'n Aqalasie'w. It got too dark to walk back around the lake. I'm sorry you got worried. I would never desert you," I responded.

Soon after, I saw my friend coming across the water. I knew Cormack would be happy now.

Chapter 17 → **MI'KMAW HOSPITALITY**

Cormack was so delighted to see the wikuom and the fire that he reminded me of a small boy going on his first hunt. With the abundance of food and hospitality, I hoped Cormack would spend a few days here resting. It made my heart feel good and a little homesick for my own village in Miawpukek.

During the night, Cormack presented James John with an offering of tobacco, and scolded me for failing to get a qalipu. I wondered what he would do if he knew I had spent the night before with the family. Cormack tried to bring the conversation around to the Beothuk people; however, we managed to distract him with Mi'kmaw songs and stories about my travels to St. John's to meet with the white man who I called Aqalasie'w, much to the delight of my friends. When asked why I called this man by such a name, I said, "If I am his Indian then he must be my White Man." At this they smiled and nodded in agreement, fully understanding that no person can own another person.

It was almost dawn when we stopped talking and singing, our bellies full. The tired feeling of the last weeks was making Cormack ready for sleep. While Cormack slept in the wikuom, James John and I went to the lakeshore. After lighting our pipes, we talked again for a long time about my journey across the island searching for our friends, the Beothuk.

I talked about my night walks to keep a lookout and to make sure the small band was not found by Cormack. I spoke again of my promise to our Elders not to lead this man to the Beothuk campsite. I wondered what would happen if we should stumble on a few wandering Beothuk who might be out on the land hunting for winter's food. It was then that my friend said the Beothuk were only about eight or nine miles away, just a day's walk from here. However, this late in the year they might be further north, at their gathering place where they were hiding for the winter months. I thanked my friend for not speaking of any of this to Cormack.

In my bundle I carried a beautiful knife. The knife had a handle carved from deer antler and had a beaded case made from deer hide; it was a precious gift given to me by the Grand Chief when I left U'nama'kik. However, I felt that it was time to pass this gift on to my friend. My friend knew as well as I, that gifts like the one I carried were never meant to be mine to keep; I was only to be the keeper and pass it on to honour a generous deed. James John had provided us with transportation, shelter, food, and information. More importantly, he would help me keep my promise to the Elders.

In our talks during the night, my friend said that a small band of Mi'kmaq was hunting to the west of our campsite. I knew that we were only about a two days' walk to the next lake to the west. That afternoon when Cormack was up and had his belly full of good food, he encouraged my friend to tell him what he knew of the trail west that would bring us to Nujioqollek. My friend talked about the trail west and drew a map on a piece of birchbark. I thanked him for his help; the trail from Miawpukek was further south and the trail west was unknown to me. I was also thankful for the information that he gave me about our brothers and sisters, the Beothuk.

It was too late in the year now for Cormack to go north. I believed he just wanted to head west to Nujioqollek as quickly as possible.

We made ready to leave my friends' warm and comfortable camp, on the day Cormack recorded as October 15, 1822. Once again, Cormack renamed this place after some person called Jameson. James John said to me in a low voice, "Who is this Jameson that he wants to name our waters after?"

"I don't know," I said, "but he already named a mountain after me. We saw Pmaqtin off in the distance along our journey from Random Bar, and he decided to call it Mount Sylvester." We both smiled and shook our heads.

The Montagnais trapper then offered to take us by gwitn to the south end of the lake, and we were happy to accept as it would save us a long walk that day. Again, our bundles were filled with smoked and dried qalipu and beaver meat, and we set off for Nujioqollek.

When we reached the south end of the lake, I said goodbye to James John and again thanked him for his great hospitality. He told us there was a small band of Mi'kmaq hunting to the west, about a two days' walk from here. Just before we went over a small hill, I looked back, and the Montagnais trapper was paddling his skin gwitn back towards his campsite.

At the end of Paqju'pe'k, which Cormack now called Jameson's Lake, we found a number of beaver houses; but since our bundles were filled with food given to us by my friend James John, there was no need to hunt.

The sky was looking darker and the trees were dark and greasy looking; the winds were coming from the northeast. Sometimes that brings big snow. I knew bad weather was coming. I said to Cormack, "We need to find a good campsite soon."

Sometime in the early afternoon a heavy snow started to fall; we were lucky to be among heavy forest with a lot of birch trees. We made camp early, and for once, Cormack helped me. In no time at all we had a comfortable shelter to crawl into. Because of the many birch trees, I was able to use birchbark to make a comfortable side tilt.

After gathering some big flat rocks to put around our fire, I collected enough wood for the night and made a big fire. Cormack asked what I was doing.

"Come in out of the snow, Indian," he said.

"The flat rocks will reflect the heat back into our tilt and help keep us warm."

Safe and warm, with plenty of wood, we settled in to weather the storm.

Chapter 19 — **MOUNT MISERY**

When the morning came there was much snow. I scraped away the snow from our firepit and was able to get a fire going again. We melted snow to make tea, and after a breakfast of tea and dried beaver meat we settled back in our shelter again. Cormack said, "There must be over three feet of snow. I don't think we can move from our camp until the snow settles."

This was one time I agreed with Cormack. The ground was not frozen and the many bog holes and brooks were covered with snow, making it dangerous to try to walk.

We spent another night in a cold camp. The trees were covered with snow and during the night a southerly wind came up and melted some of the snow. Because of the high winds many trees were falling and crashing around our campsite. "We may get crushed by the trees," I said to Cormack. I hoped we could move on soon. "The Mi'kmaw camp that James John told us about is a day's walk away, but there is much snow on the bogs, and it is dangerous to walk."

During the long day Cormack wrote on his paper. While Cormack wrote, I cut sixteen rings on my walking stick and made symbols to record our journey up to now. My journey stick was like Cormack's journal. When I returned to Miawpukek, I would present it to the Elders and they would know about the walk, who we saw, and what we saw from looking at the symbols carved into the wood. The symbols told my story to my Elders as surely as Cormack's journal told his.

Because our camp was on the lee side of the hill and under large birch trees, we were sheltered a bit from the raging storm, but it was hard to keep a fire going. The heavy snow, along with snow falling from the trees, made for a wet and miserable day and night; it was hard to dry our clothes. During the day I had time to patch my skin boots that were wearing thin. I carried with me a pair of new moccasins, which I put over my worn skin boots. Cormack looked up from his writing and looked out at the state of the forest around us. "I think I will name this place Mount Misery. What do you think of that, my Indian?"

"Good name," I thought to myself. I wondered how the Beothuk were doing in this weather; I hoped they were warm and comfortable in their winter hiding place.

After another miserable night we awoke to another stormy day. I had seventeen rings on my journey stick.

Chapter 20 → ANOTHER MI'KMAW CAMP

The next morning we got up early. After a meal of tea and bread cooked over our fire Cormack said, "The snow is going fast, today we must move from this miserable place."

All day we walked, sometimes falling down in bog and snow. We saw many qalipu, but to kill a qalipu now would be a waste. I knew there was a Mi'kmaw camp at Hatchet Pond.

After a hard walk of seven or eight miles over very

rough land, we found traps and tracks of the Mi'kmaq and soon came to the lake where a Mi'kmaw family was camped.

"Kwe! Kwe!" I heard from inside the wikuom.

"Kwe!" I responded.

"All is good to go in," I said, as Cormack pushed me aside and entered.

The wikuom was warm and comfortable inside. We greeted each other with warm hugs, as is the Mi'kmaw custom between friends and family who haven't seen each other in a long time. This small band of Mi'kmaq had come in from the west coast during the summer and was planning to move to Wapeskue'katik—known to the English as White Bear Bay—for the winter. There were many qalipu in the Wapeskue'katik area, which made for good hunting for the long winter months.

We seated ourselves on qalipu skins. Because no one spoke English, only Mi'kmaq, I translated for Cormack. *"It's going to be a long night,"* I thought.

My friends wanted to know all about the first white man they had seen on our territory. First, they wanted to know if our Grand Chief gave permission for the journey. "No," I said, "this was done by the English King's people in a place called St. John's."

Cormack asked me to explain to my friends that he was looking for the Beothuk. I explained to them in Mi'kmaq not to say much about our brothers, as they did not want to be found. There was much fear of all white men; the Beothuk were now in their winter hiding place. I explained that the Elders in Miawpukek had instructed me to not let this white man go close to the Beothuk camps, and that I had seen signs of the Beothuk along the way.

The pipe was passed around; we all smoked even though we were suffering from hunger. We could not insult my friends by refusing their generous offer of tobacco. My stomach was making noises from want of food and the comforting smell of the food cooking in a pot hung over the fire in the centre of the wikuom.

Soon it was time to eat boiled qalipu meat. I thanked my friends for the offer of food. The Chief of the camp put a small piece of meat and a pinch of tobacco on a piece of bark and went outside.

I noticed that Cormack did not eat very much. I asked, "Are you okay?"

"Yes," he said, "just my stomach is not feeling so good."

"Way too long without good cooking and good food," I thought. I was a bit concerned for Cormack; he had lost weight and now he couldn't eat much food. Maybe we would stay here for a few days to rest and get stronger

before the rest of our walk to Nujioqollek. But when the Mi'kmaq said to Cormack that it would take another ten days to reach the coast, he wanted to leave as soon as possible.

Chapter 21 → GIFTS OF THE LAND

fter a two-day rest with good food and a warm place to sleep, we were eager to continue our journey to Nujioqollek. The land to the west was all high hills and not a lot of forest, just low spruce trees. However, the land in some places was red with partridgeberries. The early autumn snowfall had covered the berries for a few days and made them taste sweet. We picked as many as we could to mix with our flour when we stopped for the day. Partridge-berries would make a refreshing drink if we came across some balsam fir trees; the tips mixed with partridgeberries would be a good tonic.

That day we saw lots of qalipu but did not bother to take one. Later that day we saw a mui'n on a distant hillside, feasting on the berries. I said to Cormack, "The bear is getting fat for the long winter months. That bear would provide great meat and lots of fat for our journey."

We decided to walk around a low hill to get downwind from the mui'n. Once we were within range for our musket, we shot the mui'n and cleaned it, then set up camp close by. The mui'n was very fat and must have weighed two or three hundred pounds. I explained to Cormack, "Bear meat is great, and it won't hurt your stomach like other meat. It's almost as good as beaver and very good for travel. We will not be hungry all day."

Cormack decided that we would camp for another two days to feast on the mui'n meat and fat. I said to Cormack, "Winter is very close. We are up on the high country now."

But Cormack just said, "We camp for two days to rest." I thought to myself that Cormack must be getting tired.

After a great supper of roasted mui'n, we made a big fire and slept like two babies. I awoke early and looked over at Cormack. He was still sleeping so I went out to put more wood on the fire. Some of the mui'n meat hung on a stick not far from the fire, so I cooked more meat. Cormack woke and came to the fire. He said, "You are a real glutton."

I asked, "What is 'glutton'?"

"You are eating too much. That will make you sick."

I said, "Bear meat is very good. The fat from this bear is as white as the feathers of a partridge. This bear lived on good country food. Bear fat is also good medicine." Cormack just shook his head and went back to his blanket.

I sat by the fire, just to smoke my pipe and be in the beauty of the place. As I sat there, I wondered what hardships lay ahead for us. We were about ten days from the west coast, but bad weather and heavy snow could make the journey even longer. Cormack came out and sat by the fire. He, too, took out his pipe and sat on the ground across from me. He looked worried.

"How much do you know about this family that has treated us to great hospitality? Do they really know anything about the Beothuk we are trying to find?" he asked.

Not knowing what to say, I smoked my pipe and thought about how to answer Cormack's questions as honestly as I could.

"First," I said, "these good people are hard workers and look after their family. In your world, your people might say these are poor people and maybe call them savages. Their wikuoms are plenty comfortable, and they have lots of good food to eat. And most important, they are willing to share their comfort and food with strangers. This family is rich because they have shelter and much good food."

"If this family went to your town," I continued, "would the people invite them into their big houses and feed them? We do not notice how their camp and clothes smell different than your clothes did when we first met in your town. Their clothes smell like the land and the life they live. Wikuoms smell smoky. Clothes smell like the pelts that they clean and work with every day.

"You say we have no Bible, and we are looked upon as what you call 'savages'. But your people kill our people for money or to take away our land and food sources. When you block our rivers and take our fish and access to other foods we need, our people get weak; they cannot fight with weak bodies. Nursing mothers' milk dries up from lack of food that we need." Cormack did not say anything, but he stared at me in a strange way. So I continued to tell my story of our survival on this rugged land.

I said to Cormack, "You think you are rich because you buy your foods and live in fancy houses. We believe this land we walk on is our Bible. This land gives us all that we need—clothes to keep us warm, food for our survival, transportation, and shelter from the cold. Most of all, it teaches us how to be humble, have patience, and have much respect for all the good things the Great Spirit has given us. Does your Bible tell you such things? Your people may think of us as lazy and having no God and no spiritual guidance. When this family shared their food and shelter with us, did you not see the head man of this family take food outside? That was done to give thanks for the good fortune and the blessing of life and strength, which comes from the comfort and feeling of happiness knowing your land and family are safe, if only for this moment. In life, we only have moments. There will always be much laughter in our wikuoms because laughter is good for the heart and spirit."

Cormack looked at me for a long time. I thought he was angry, but then he said, "You are right. Your friends would not be very welcome in our town because they are Indian."

For a long time, we sat and smoked our pipes. Then I said, "They tell me that our Beothuk brothers are all gone to the north for the winter. Soon the big snows will come, and the big lakes will be frozen for many moons."

Chapter 22 → CIRCLE OF LIFE

For two days we feasted. The next morning we noticed winter was setting in. The smaller ponds were frozen. Ducks and geese were all gone south, and the partridge had white feathers. I thought the trail to the west would not be easy from that point on. Before we left our campsite, I stored the remaining meat and bearskin in a tall rock formation just in case someone might come along and need food. The rock formation would let travellers know there was food under the rocks.

Cormack asked many questions about the land ahead. I could only tell him that I had never walked this far west before, but I knew the walking would be bad and maybe dangerous. Low spruce on the ground covered deep holes, and the low brush would make for rough walking. Cormack talked about taming the qalipu to pull a sled like they do in some country called Norway. I thought I would like to see Cormack try to get a big qalipu to pull his sled, especially during mating time. *"Just like the Englishmen,"* I thought, *"always wanting to tame a magical spiritual animal like the qalipu."* To watch the qalipu run and prance across a bog, at times it looked like the animal was floating on air.

During the day Cormack talked about how those qalipu could be tamed and could create work for people. The Laplanders could come and tame the herds and slaughter the meat for people that live along the coast. Cormack said that if the Indians didn't want to do this work, or were too lazy or unfit, then the Laplanders could do it.

I thought to myself, *"This I would not want to see. That sounds a lot like what happened all over Turtle Island, the place that the white men call North America."*

The white man came many years ago: first they stole our lands, then they called us savages and tried to tame us. Now this man Cormack says he would like to tame the beautiful free-ranging qalipu. *"What next?"* I wondered.

On our journey west we saw hundreds of qalipu going towards the east. They were coming down off the barrens where they spent the summer with their calves. It was now late October and all the herds were heading east and south to spend the winter months where food was easier to get, mostly because the snow was not as deep. Plenty of qalipu moved closer to our people; the Mi'kmaw family would live well this winter. Cormack told me that that movement is called a 'migration'.

"We call this the circle of life," I told him.

I knew that I would have to explain to him the meaning of my words. "The qalipu roam free and live on the land just like our people used to, but now not as much. The qalipu move to winter grounds, which makes it easy for our people to get food for the long winter and spring. Our people are part of this circle of life as well."

"In the spring there will be many young qalipu," I continued, "Then, the qalipu will move to summer grounds. In the spring, qalipu hide is only good for babiche—for making snowshoes."

"Why is this?" Cormack asked.

"Because," I said, "in the winter the qalipu have big maggots in their hide, which leave big holes.

"In your world, you keep cattle and sheep inside a

fence. Your people kill those animals for food. That is your circle," I said.

Cormack did not say anything for a long time. He just nodded his head and wrote on his paper.

Chapter 23 — **WE SUFFER FROM OUR LONG WALK AND WINTER MOVING IN**

Cormack said it was October 29. I knew that the trail ahead would be hard because of the winter season moving in. This would make for hard walking and our bodies would suffer greatly from exhaustion. I told Cormack that if we had taken the time to smoke and dry the bear meat to carry with us, our bodies would be much stronger, having good food to eat and being well-rested from the break in travel.

Walking all day, sometimes falling and stumbling in

bog holes covered with snow, was making us tired. Days were getting shorter and it was much colder at night. Because the trees in the area were nothing more than low bushes, some nights we couldn't even get enough dry wood to have a fire. We spent many nights cold and miserable, and at times we did not even have a dry place to make camp. Because of cold and wet camps, we couldn't dry our clothes at night, which made for long, tiring days. Our skin boots were starting to wear through, and our clothes were ragged with holes worn through in many places. The clothes we had started out with were not really fit for winter.

I told Cormack that there should be a Mi'kmaw camp not far from where we were, maybe a walk of one or two days. We came up on another big lake; Cormack called this lake Wilson's Lake, in honour of his friend from some place called Edinburgh in his own land. I didn't bother to tell him the real name of the lake; he is a stubborn man anyway.

Later that day we crossed a fast-flowing river that runs down to the south coast. The water was cold. Cormack said, "I think winter has caught up to us." Cormack called this river Little River. He asked if this was the last one between us and the south coast, but I was too tired and cold to say yes or no; I just wanted to get warm. *"Miawpukek would be a great place to be,"* I thought.

Soon, we saw smoke rising above the treetops. Smoke

means fire, warmth, and good food. The smoke was coming from the other side of the lake. Cormack said, "It must be a timber party from St. George's Bay."

I thought, *"No timber party in this far. This must be a Mi'kmaw family trapping and hunting for their winter's food."*

We walked down to the edge of the lake. We could see the wikuom through the trees. There was smoke coming from the wikuom and a small fire burned outside. No one showed themselves. "Maybe they are scared," I said. By this time, we were looking rough and ragged from our long travels.

At first Cormack was waving his arms in the air like a crazy person. I said, "Maybe they are Mi'kmaq and you make them scared. Let me speak to them." I yelled, "KWE! KWE!" Soon two young girls came to the edge of the lake. I spoke to them in my language and told them who we were.

"We are travellers from the east coast. This white man with me is Cormack. We are not lost but would like to visit and get warm and share stories of our travels. The aqalasie'w is looking for the Beothuk," I told them, "our brothers, the Beothuk. If you know of them, please don't tell this man anything."

I said all this in Mi'kmaq and the girls answered back that their father was out hunting for the day.

Cormack asked, "Are they talking about me and our journey?"

"No," I said. "They just didn't know who we were. I think you scared them when you were waving your arms and shouting."

"I didn't mean to scare anyone. I was merely trying to get their attention."

I yelled to the girls, "Could you come over and bring us to your camp? We mean you no harm."

When Cormack saw them put the skin gwitn in the water, he looked pleased again. He said something that I couldn't understand, but I didn't care. I was going to speak my language again. My heart hurt from having to talk to Cormack in English over the past weeks.

When the Mi'kmaw girls landed on the shore, Cormack held his hand up in the air and said, "I mean you no harm." The poor girls had no idea what he was saying. The gwitn was covered with qalipu skins like the gwitn we used to cross the lake with James John, but much bigger. The girls told me that there were eight people in their family: their father, four women, and three children.

When we walked into the warm wikuom, the smell of food and comfort was so great that it made me homesick for my own family. I was so happy that none of the people in the camp could speak a word of English. My heart soared to hear my language; it was like hearing my grandmother singing in the early morning as she happily prepared breakfast for me and Grandfather before we went out on the land.

The young women said that they left Nujioqollek three moons ago. They came here because there was good shelter, lots of good firewood, and plenty of qalipu. Cormack looked around the wikuom as if he was not sure whether he was permitted to sit. I explained to the women that he could not understand our language, but I could explain their words to him. The women said that their father would be back soon; then we would talk. Now we could have tea, qalipu stew, and lu'skinikin roasted over the fire—a feast after our long walk.

Cormack saw the small baby for the first time. The little one was strapped in a cradleboard and was placed upright against the side of the wikuom. The baby was asleep. As I gazed at the baby, I wondered if the family would one day tell the story of this time in their life when a wild, ragged aqalasie'w and a Mi'kmaw called Sylvester spent a moment in time in their lives so long ago.

Cormack said, "How sad to have that baby stuck up like a piece of furniture."

"The baby is not crying and is very comfortable. Cradleboards have been used by my people long before your people arrived on our land," I said to him. "Would you like me to speak to the mother and tell her you are not happy with where she placed the baby?"

Cormack's eyes opened wide and he said, "No! I meant no harm. I am just curious."

Soon Gabriel, the girls' father, came home from his hunt and his two daughters ran out to meet him. I could hear the girls telling him in Mi'kmaq that there was a white man and a Mi'kmaw inside. Gabriel stepped into the wikuom and spoke to his family first, asking them if everyone was okay. They all said yes. Then he went to the cradleboard and hugged the little one. Then he turned and spoke to me. "Good to see you, Sylvester. Tell me news of your family."

At this point Cormack tried to speak but I said, "No, you are in this man's house now. If you were away and came back to your house and there was a strange man there with your family, what would you do? Just sit down until Gabriel and I finish talking. Then I will tell him your words."

"Who is this aqalasie'w you bring to my wikuom?" Gabriel asked.

I assured him that this aqalasie'w was okay and that I had walked with him for many weeks. I gave him the same warning about the Beothuk as I had given his daughters. Gabriel agreed with me and my Elders; he would not tell anything he knew about our brothers and sisters, the Beothuk people.

Letting Cormack into the conversation, I started speaking in both Mi'kmaq and English. "He is looking for the Beothuk but now we are too far south and low on food, and our skin boots are worn. How many days to the coast?" I asked.

"The Beothuk are all gone to their winter camp. Unless you want to spend the winter in the woods, you should leave soon for the west coast," Gabriel said. "I could show you a good trail to the coast. My family can stay here until I come back; we have plenty of food and Mi'kmaw women are good hunters and trappers."

I explained all this to Cormack, and he agreed to accept Gabriel's offer to lead the way west to Nujioqollek.

Gabriel's wife gave us new qalipu skin boots. I took mine and put them on at once, but Cormack refused them. "No, mine are fine," he said, not knowing that to refuse such a gift was a great insult.

I explained to Cormack, "Take the gift and put them in your bundle. That way you will not insult these good people." I gave thanks to the Great Spirit that the Mi'kmaw family did not understand English. If Cormack insulted Gabriel's wife, he might decide not to show us the trail to Nujioqollek.

Gabriel said he would leave two guns and plenty of ammunition and powder; the women could provide for themselves while he was away. Gabriel said we should leave the camp in a few hours. While we sat and talked about the walk and trail ahead, one young girl returned with some fresh qalipu meat from her hunt. It was immediately added to the pot. We feasted on roasted qalipu tongue and fat qalipu meat. For a while I wished that Gabriel could speak a little English. Then he could also explain the travelling to Cormack, just as I did. Travelling too far north this late in the year would be hard walking.

Chapter 24 → THROUGH SNOW AND ICE

Early in the day—on October 30, 1822, according to Cormack—rain, snow, and high winds forced us to stop and make camp. Gabriel shot a hare. Like the winter, the hare was snow white. Gabriel saw the big arctic hare first and pointed it out to us; just the tips of his ears and his tail were black. We feasted that night on hare roasted over the fire. The meat was a bit tough, but we ate it. Then we built up our fire and crawled into our shelter, hoping that the next day would be better.

The next morning, after a restless night, Gabriel and I walked out from the campsite to find lumps of snow. We knew that under those lumps there were partridge. We came back to the campsite with several partridge for our breakfast. Cormack was sitting beside the fire. When he saw the birds he said, "Where did you get those? I didn't hear a gunshot."

We explained the birds were under the snow, and we just had to walk up and pluck them out from under the snow. After cleaning the partridge, we roasted enough for our breakfast and took the rest in our bundles for our journey that day.

The next day, we left our campsite. We had camped in a small island of woods. I looked several times and wondered if the trail ahead was going to offer us better sites than this one. During the day we saw plenty of qalipu but chose not to shoot one. Gabriel said there was plenty of qalipu along the trail so we should be good for food, plus there were plenty of big rabbits.

That day we decided to try our luck and walk along the shoreline. The ponds were now frozen over. As we walked on the ice I talked to Gabriel. Walking the land with him and speaking our language made me feel like I was home. I was so happy to be speaking Mi'kmaq again, especially after all those weeks struggling to speak English so that Cormack could understand what I was trying to tell him. More and more I thought that Cormack was not a bad man, but new to the customs of our people and the struggles to survive on this land. My hope for him was that he could learn from our people.

Lost in thought, I was not paying attention and I fell through the ice. When my feet touched bottom, I pushed to the surface and crawled out onto the ice. Gabriel stood and laughed at me. Meanwhile Cormack just stood there with a shocked look on his face.

"Why didn't your friend help you?" Cormack asked.

"You say I'm your Indian. Gabriel thought you would help. He didn't want to make you angry."

Later, I talked with Gabriel in Mi'kmaq, telling him that Cormack asked why he did not help me. Gabriel replied, "I knew you didn't need help because the water was only shallow. I would have helped you if you needed it." We laughed together when Gabriel said, "You had a funny look on your face. Cold water made you take a big breath. Now we make a fire and dry your clothes." Cormack took his new skin boots out of his pack and offered them to me. I nodded and accepted his gift.

Chapter 25 — KING GEORGE THE FOURTH'S LAKE

The next day, we crossed between two rivers running northeast. Gabriel said the rivers were the main source branches of the Sple'tk. The river runs almost two hundred miles. We saw many qalipu that day and shot a nice fat barren doe. It was breeding time for the qalipu; the male qalipu were in rut and not good for food, but the doe had never had a calf. It was good fat meat for our journey.

Almost a foot of snow was now on the ground; the world around us was a sea of white. The snow covered all the low vegetation and made walking very difficult. We camped that night at the southern end of a lake. Gabriel said this was the southerly boundary for the Beothuk, and the source of Sple'tk. From this lake our people and the Beothuk started and ended the water journey to the west coast.

Gabriel told us it was on this site that the Mi'kmaq made their first qalipu skin gwitn. Over the years many gwitns were left here for other Mi'kmaq and sometimes the Beothuk would take the skin gwitns. Sometimes in later years the Beothuk would take just the skin of the gwitn that was left at this landing place. "How do you know the Beothuk take the gwitn skins?" Cormack asked.

"Because they always leave a gift. Sometimes they leave a skin pouch filled with red ochre and other times a bone carving," Gabriel said. Gabriel showed Cormack the bone carving hanging on a qalipu-hide string around his neck.

From this spot, walking to the coast was by far the easier way to travel. Gabriel said to me, "It is only about twenty-five miles to Nujioqollek. There are no other big lakes from here to the coast." Cormack announced he was naming this lake in honour of the king of his country,

George the Fourth. *"Who is this king Cormack talks about and gives away land and water?"* I wondered. *"Our Kji' Saqamaw should know about this."*

For nearly twenty miles to the west of the lake, which Cormack named George the Fourth, the land was barren with hardly enough wood to make a fire at night. It made bad walking during the day, and our clothes were ragged and torn from the low underbrush.

On the first day of Cormack's month of November, we crossed over two rapid rivers running west into Nujioqollek. Along the way we had seen hundreds of qalipu west of the lake, but as we neared the coast very few were seen. Gabriel said to me, "That is why our people move inland where there are many qalipu and good trapping."

While going down a mountain, I felt overjoyed to be near to the coast. I felt stronger; my spirit was happy, my heart was happy, and in some way, I felt a kind of sorrow that this journey would soon be over.

We sat on the hillside, all three of us. I believed Cormack was happy and showed a little respect for our abilities to survive on the harsh land. Cormack said, "I feel so much stronger now, maybe more now than any time in my life."

"Mi'kmaq feel that way every day," I said. "The land which we walk on while speaking our language is all good for the heart and spirit."

Sitting there on the hillside, Cormack looked at me and said, "You are a good Indian."

Chapter 26 → # THE SEA AT LAST, AND MI'KMAW HOSPITALITY ONCE AGAIN

T hat evening, almost eighteen miles west of George the Fourth Lake, from the top of the snow-covered ridge we could see the sea; what a beautiful sight. All three of us just stood there for the longest time taking in the sight and the beautiful wonders of Mother Nature. We saw Nujioqollek from our snowy hilltop. Cormack said, "It would have been so much better if we had gotten here a month sooner. I need to catch a ship going to St. John's."

I turned to Gabriel and said, "I think my aqalasie'w just started crying. I don't know if he is happy or sad that our journey is almost over. I think that when I get to Nujioqollek, after a good rest, I will go back to Miawpukek to have council with my Elders and report all that I saw on this long walk."

I looked at the sea and Nujioqollek. There was not a bit of snow anywhere. But when I looked back from where we came, all was covered with snow. On the hilltop I felt like we were between two worlds: one of pure white behind us, and another in front of us—the vast sea. Many emotions came over me.

We prepared ourselves for the difficult journey down to the bay. The mountain we stood on was very high above sea level. Cormack said it was two thousand feet or more. I questioned whether Cormack would know such a thing as that. I asked my friend in Mi'kmaq, "How high are we from the sea?"

"I don't know, but it's a long way down and not easy. I call this place Mntua'gi—Devil's Place, or Hard Place to Go Down or Up."

The trail down was hard and dangerous. At the bottom of the mountain there was a fast-flowing river called Flat Bay River. Gabriel said, "We must cross the river and make camp on the other side. It looks like rain and if big rain comes, this river will swell very high and fast."

By the afternoon of the following day, we were at the river. As Gabriel predicted, it was wide and fast at this point. I looked back up at the mountain and was amazed that we had made it down without more than a few scratches and bruised legs and arms. Now Gabriel said, "We make a raft, or we walk across the river."

We decided to take the walk across. I used my walking stick to help keep me from falling in the river. Gabriel said to me, "We should put heavy rocks in our bundles to help keep our feet on the bottom of the river. But if you fall, throw off your bundle or you will drown."

We cut a long pole to make a walking stick for Cormack. We strapped our muskets across our packs and stepped into the cold, fast-flowing river. Step after step, we made it across the river. My legs and half my body were numb with cold. I looked at Cormack; he was shaking, and his lips were blue. I said to Gabriel, "There is lots of good wood on this side of the river. We make camp and make a big fire. We will get warm and get hot food and dry clothes."

Chapter 27 → THE END OF THE JOURNEY

"Tomorrow we should reach Nujioqollek," Gabriel said. I was very happy that this strong Mi'kmaw had decided to come along on this part of our journey. I said to him in Mi'kmaq, "Thank you my friend, for taking the time away from your family."

The next morning, we walked along the bank of Flat Bay River. There was lots of good wood in this area. Cormack said, "This forest reminds me of the forest in Nova Scotia."

On that same day we reached Nujioqollek. According to Gabriel, the first two houses we saw close to the shore belonged to Mi'kmaw families. The houses were barred and nailed up for the season.

Gabriel said, "Those families have been gone now for months, trapping and hunting qalipu, bear, and beaver. They spend up to three moons inland, smoke-drying their meat for the winter."

The Europeans' houses were located on the west side of the harbour. Cormack had friends there and was looking for transportation back to St. John's. However, the distance across this part of the bay was about a mile wide and a strong westerly wind prevented us from crossing. Not having had much food for two days, Cormack said, "We should break open the door of one of the houses." He walked towards one of the houses, and broke open the door for us.

Once inside, I asked Gabriel if he knew who owned the house. He said with a smile, "This is the Chief's house."

I turned to Cormack and said, "This house belongs to the Chief. His name is Edmund Gontgont. But we need food and it looks like there are plenty of vegetables and six barrels of fish." We found pickled fish of many kinds, dried salted codfish, seal oil in bladders, two barrels of corn flour, and a small bottle of black molasses.

Because of the windstorm, we stayed overnight in the Chief's house. Because we broke into the house, we were obligated to stay and protect the property. It was decided that even if Cormack chose to leave before the Chief came back, out of honour to our Mi'kmaw brother, Gabriel and I would stay and explain our reasons.

A few days later, a party of Mi'kmaq arrived from inland—men and women carrying loads of fur. The Chief was not pleased to find his door broken and his home occupied by an aqalasie'w. The Chief said to Cormack, "If I was here in my house and you broke my door and came in and ate my food—what would you do if I did that to your house?"

I quickly explained in Mi'kmaq to the Chief what we were doing in his house and that we had walked for two moons. I told the Chief that Cormack was looking for the Beothuk, but we didn't find them. We spoke in Mi'kmaq, so Cormack didn't know that I told the Chief the whole story of our journey.

The next day we crossed the harbour, but before Cormack left the Chief's house, he offered to pay for the damaged door and the food we had eaten. In true Mi'kmaw way, the Chief refused any offer of payment. When I walked out the door, the Chief said to me, "If you weren't here

Sylvester, maybe we would have pickled aqalasie'w for the winter." We chuckled and he hugged me and said, "Come back, Sylvester. We have much to talk about. That is one aqalasie'w—soon we will see many more."

I said goodbye to my friends and promised to come back again. Cormack was standing outside waiting for me and he asked me what the Chief said to me. I looked him in the eye and said, "He is coming to visit your house soon."

When we got to the other side of the harbour, Cormack was received by his friends, Jersey and English, with open arms. Cormack was told that all ships had left the harbour a month ago and because of the lateness of the fall season, there was no chance for him to get passage to St. John's. Cormack offered large amounts of money to get someone to bring him to Fortune Bay on the south coast, where he hoped to catch a ship still in the harbour, but there was no one available.

Chapter 28 → CORMACK PARTS WITH HIS INDIAN

We sat in Cormack's friend's house and talked long into the night. At times we stopped talking for many minutes, quietly smoking our pipes. Finally, Cormack said, "I need to go to the south coast to get a ship back to St. John's, or to another country, since there are no ships sailing from here."

Cormack looked surprised when I said, "You can come with me. We can go to Gabriel's camp, then travel on to Najioponuk. From there it will be much easier to get a ship to St. John's."

"No, Sylvester, I don't think I can make that journey overland. It may take too long with the winter coming on. There is much snow in the interior, and I don't have clothes for winter travel. My offer to you, Sylvester, is still good. I can take you with me to Spain or Portugal. You can come with me and we can possibly find transportation for you to Bay d'Espoir from somewhere on our journey on the west coast."

I thanked Cormack, but I was ready to finish this journey that I had started months ago. With a little sadness in my heart, I left this strange white man behind.

Afterword

SPECULATION

Very little is known about Sylvester Joe beyond Cormack's journal. Oral histories suggest that after leaving Cormack in 1822, Sylvester may have gone in search of the Beothuk winter camp. There are stories that Sylvester did come back to Miawpukek in the spring of 1823 for a few weeks, but left again one morning at dawn to travel to the west country.

We do know that Sylvester was around Miawpukek again in 1828, because at that time Cormack asked Sylvester to accompany him to the gravesite on Mekwe'jite'wa'kik—Red Indian Lake—to look for the remains of the Beothuk man and woman killed by Europeans. One was shot on the ice by the Peytons in 1819; the other died by disease and transport in 1820. Sylvester refused to accompany Cormack. Later that year Sylvester left Miawpukek and was never seen again.

William Cormack did go back to Red Indian Lake, and there he removed the skulls of Nonosabasut and Demasduit from their burial hut. In 1828, Cormack took the skulls back to Scotland for study, where they remained until 2020.

SEPARATION

There is a legend that is well-known through Mi'kmaq oral history about how the Beothuk and the Mi'kmaq lived together harmoniously on the west coast of Newfoundland, at Seal Rocks, St. George's Bay/Nujioqollek. One version of the story *How the Micmac and the Red Indians Became Separated* (Narrated by John Paul at Badger's Brook) is documented in Frank G. Speck's book *Beothuk and Micmac*. This harmonious coexistence came to an end, as the story goes, over an unfortunate incident involving a black weasel.

In Speck's version, the Mi'kmaw boy kills the weasel and subsequently kills a Beothuk boy. In the version known to Mi'sel Joe, the Beothuk boy kills the weasel and kills the Mi'kmaw boy.

Speck's version, as given in his book, is as follows:

"Long ago the Micmac and the Red Indians were friendly and lived together in a village at St. George's Bay, which is now supposed to have been near Seal rocks [near Stevensville]. The place was called *Meski'gtuwi'den*, 'big gut,' or it might have been *Nudjo'-yan*, inside Sandy point in the bay. The St. George's river was at that time called Main River by the English. Everything went well between the two tribes. They used to have a large gwitn at the village in which the people could cross over the bay. One time during the winter a Micmac boy killed a black weasel. As it was winter-time the weasel should, of course, have been white. The occurrence was taken as an omen of misfortune, because the boy should not have killed a black weasel in winter-time, the animal not being in its proper hue. On account of the violation of the taboo a quarrel arose between the boys who were at the time gathered near the big gwitn already mentioned. The Micmac boy struck and killed a Red Indian boy and left him there. Soon the Red Indian boy was missed by his people, and after searching for several days they found his body lying near the big gwitn. When they examined the wounds the Red Indians concluded that the boy had been murdered. They accused the Micmac of doing the deed, and in a few days feeling became so intense that a fight ensued in which the Red Indians were beaten and driven out. They retreated into the interior and, being separated from contact with the outside world, drifted into barbarism and became wilder. They always shunned the Micmac, who soon after obtained firearms and, although they never persecuted the Red Indians, were thenceforth objects of terror to them. In a few generations those of the two tribes who were able to converse together died out and there was no way left for them to come together. So living in fear of each other, yet avoiding clashes, the Micmac continued to live at Bay St. George and the Red Indians kept to the interior."

—As narrated by John Paul at Badger's Brook, in Frank Speck's Beothuk and Micmac, in the collection Indian Notes and Monographs: A series of publications relating to the American Aborigines. (See References for full citation.)

Chief Mi'sel Joe's perspective on the story, September 2020:

There is no way of knowing what's true and what's fiction because this happened so many hundreds of years ago, and the story gets told and retold. Mi'kmaw people across the island are telling versions of the same story, and sometimes adding their own narrative. The story changes with the storyteller.

Nobody knows if it's factual, but it's a story that has been around for hundreds of years. Somebody didn't just make it up; this story is part of the oral history of the Mi'kmaw people.

Omens have been part of our way of life. Mi'kmaw people believed in omens, and still do today. Like spirit travel or casting a spell, whether it be a good spell or a bad spell, we believe it could be done and it's still being done. I've seen it work when I was growing up, and I continue to see it today. The story about the weasel being the wrong colour in the wrong season is an omen that we would recognize today. If we were on the land in the winter and saw a black weasel, we would know it was the wrong colour for the season and it would be an omen of some kind. We would watch for it. You don't know what you're watching for, but something is not right with nature. Two or three hundred years ago, we were closer to nature than we are today; we were part of nature. And anything that wasn't right, like the weasel, was a sign that something wasn't right. A current example of how nature can sometimes give you a kick in the gut and make you take notice would be "Snowmageddon", the massive blizzard that hit the City of St. John's in January 2020 and shut the city down for eight days. We call it climate change, but it's still Mother Nature's way of telling us that we are doing something wrong, and we take notice.

Another example is the tidal wave that caused havoc on the south coast in 1929 and is still being talked about today. It wiped out some small communities. It left people hungry and without medical attention. From a Mi'kmaw perspective, that would be a wake-up call. I remember it because my grandfather's workshop got flooded. The high water came all the way from the Burin Peninsula into the Bay d'Espoir and other coastal communities. But it did not hit those areas as bad as it hit Burin.

Weasels, like other animals, mark the seasons. Partridge turns white in winter months and brown in the summer. Same with rabbits and qalipu. Our people watch for this. If the qalipu turn white early in the season, then we know it's going to be an early winter. Our people watch nature and judge nature on the kind of winter we will have. One indication of nature telling us what kind of winter is coming is the beaver lodge. If it has lots of brouse (vegetation) around it, there is going to be a lot of snow and it will be a bit of a rough winter. So the omen of the black weasel in the wrong season was an omen that something bad was going to happen. It is a sacred twist of nature, actually.

In the case of two different cultures, the Beothuk and the Mi'kmaq, it may not have meant the same to both groups to see a weasel not changing with the seasons. The Beothuk may not have the same belief in omens as the Mi'kmaq do, and that may have caused the harsh departure of the two groups. If the Beothuk and Mi'kmaq had the same teachings about omens, then nothing would have happened to the weasel or the little boy.

REPATRIATION

In 1828, the skulls of Nonosabasut, who had been murdered by John Peyton in 1819, and his wife Demasduit, who died of tuberculosis as a result of contact with Europeans in 1820, were removed from their gravesite on Red Indian Lake by William Cormack and brought to Scotland for study.

Chief Mi'sel Joe began the repatriation of these Beothuk remains in 2014. I asked him to speak about it, in his own words, as something we could include in *My Indian*. Having worked with him in the writing of this book since July 2017, our discussion became very raw and personal. As a distant relative of Sylvester Joe, Chief Joe's successful repatriation of the remains from Edinburgh, Scotland, to St. John's, Newfoundland and Labrador, on March 11, 2020, brings the story of *My Indian* full circle. The following is based on my recollection of our discussion.

July 11, 2020 at the Chief's kitchen table, over a cup of tea:

"Interest began when I was asked to be part of the Beothuk Institute, about twenty years ago. William Cormack originally founded the Beothuk Institute in 1827, and it was revised by artist Gerry Squires and incorporated in St. John's in 1997. The Beothuk Institute commissioned the statue, the *Spirit of the Beothuk*, in Boyd's Cove. The remains in Scotland were talked about then, but the Beothuk Institute chose not to pursue repatriation.

"In 2014, I decided to go to Scotland to see the remains for myself, as a Mi'kmaq Chief from Miawpukek First Nation. First, I sent a letter to the National Museum of Scotland to introduce myself and give them some history on Miawpukek First Nation. I followed this up with a phone call to the museum. Later that fall, I decided to go and talk with people at the museum and see the remains.

"When I went to the museum, I was told I could not see the remains. I decided to stay and visit the museum but was determined that next year I would come back and I would see them. When leaving, I joked that if I didn't see the remains next year, I was going to dig up Robbie Burns and bring him back to Newfoundland and Labrador for study.

"In 2015 I went back again and that time I did see some

remains. I was led into a small room, maybe ten feet by ten feet. They had four people accompany me. I asked if I could be alone with the remains, but they said no. The compromise was that only one person would stay with me, and the others left. I saw *some* remains; I have no way of knowing if they were the actual Beothuk. They had sweetgrass there; someone who was there before had done a sweetgrass ceremony with some remains. They couldn't remember who, or what nation they came from. I used their sweetgrass that had been left behind. I felt it was amazing that they had sweetgrass left there, like it had been left there for me to use.

"They all had white gloves on while they uncovered the remains. I asked if I could touch and was told no. But I did put my fingers very lightly on one of the skulls. I could feel all sorts of emotions going through my body, and I actually started to cry. I don't know if I was saying hello or saying goodbye. I felt a spiritual, emotional connection that seemed to go on for a long time, but probably was only seconds. It felt like a long, drawn-out moment.

"My vision of the room went blank. I had no vision of anybody else in the room or the room itself. Only me and those skulls. I had a deep, deep sense of sorrow. The only time I have ever felt that deep, deep sorrow was when our son drowned. He was only eight years old.

"That feeling wasn't there when the remains returned to Newfoundland and Labrador. I was happy. Maybe it was a different kind of happy since they were home—on their way back home to their final resting place.

"My emotions were somewhat spoiled by the media that was there and the flaunting of a book written about the Beothuk people. A much more private ceremony with just the five (Indigenous) leaders and the premier would have been much more appropriate. And sacred.

"When a member of your family passes away, you don't invite strangers and the media. These are sacred remains. Having all those people in the room took away from the remains being on their way home. The Rooms in St. John's is just a stopover.

"It was a happy moment, but a sad moment in that we couldn't do it in a more private setting."

—Chief Mi'sel Joe, in conversation with Sheila O'Neill

APPENDICES

GLOSSARY
Mi'kmaq to English

General vocabulary:

Aqalasie'w	English person, white man
Babiche	Strips of qalipu hide used for lacings to make snowshoes, clothing
Gwitn	Canoe; maskwiey canoe is a birchbark canoe
Keselul	I love you
Kitpu	Eagle
Kwe	Hello
Lpa'tu'jij	Small boy
Lu'skinikin	Indian bread made with bear fat and sometimes blueberries, roasted over an open fire
Maskwiey	Birchbark
Mi'kmaq (plural)	My friends; Mi'kmaw is the singular form, and is also an adjective
Mntua'gi	Devil's Place
Mui'n	Bear
Nei'n	My
Pitaoukuog	Beothuk, meaning people who lived upriver
Pjilasi	Welcome
Qalipu	Caribou

Saqamaw	Chief
Kji' Saqamaw	Grand Chief. The Grand Chief is head of the Mi'kmaw nation. The Mi'kmaw nation is made up of seven districts, which extend from Newfoundland all the way to Quebec and parts of the United States.
Suliewey	Silver; Sylvester's Mi'kmaw name, given for the silver streak in his hair
Wikuom	Wigwam
Wuklatmu'jk	Little People. Ancient stories tell of little people that came around when you left tobacco and gifts for them on the mountain. When your body was free of chemicals and negative emotions, the Wuklatmu'jk would come around and visit you. They were always invisible; you couldn't see them but you always knew they were there. Once or twice a year people would do a fast to maintain a good connection with their spirit protector. The Wuklatmu'jk would stay with them the entire time.
	In modern times, the only time you will see the Wuklatmu'jk now is when you do a fast for four days and your body is free of modern-day influences like television,

Wuklatmu'jk (cont'd) telephones, alcohol, coffee, tea. When your spirit is free, your heart is free, and your soul is free, the Wuklatmu'jk will come around. They will stay with you until your body becomes influenced by those modern-day things once again. Sometimes they play tricks on you. (Mi'sel Joe)

Cultural concepts and artifacts:

Kesite'tasiklmuni'l Medicine Bundle. Sylvester's medicine bundle would have included a repair kit for sewing and ground-up medicines from the land. He would have had bear grease, a kitpu feather, and a small bit of red ochre. He would also have a tiny piece of tanned qalipu hide for patching his boots or clothing, and a small piece of red cloth, which he might use to mark something sacred. (Mi'sel Joe)

Seven Sorts The 'seven sorts' is the name of a magical medicine made up of seven plants (cherry bark, alder bark, dogwood bark, yellow root, beaver root, ground juniper and balsam fir tips) that are boiled down and made into a salve. This salve was used on the body to cure serious injuries. There is a teaching revolving around the seven virtues of life; the number seven has always been a magical number for the Mi'kmaq. For example, seven plants are used in the Sweat Lodge. They don't have to be the same plants used to make up the Seven Sorts, but will usually include balsam fir and wild cherry bark.

Place names:

Ktaqamkuk/Taqamkuk	The island of Newfoundland. Taqamkuk is used when one is not on the island; Ktaqamkuk is used when one is on the island
Lapite'spe'l	Bay d'Espoir
Lu'tik	Roti Bay
Mekwaye'Katik	Middle Ridge
Mekwe'jite'wa'kik	Red Indian Lake
Miawpukek	Middle River; Mi'kmaq name for First Nations reserve in Conne River (established in 1897)

Mikl'n	Miquelon
Mntua'gi	Devil's Place
Najioponuk	Burgeo
Nujioqollek	St. George's Bay
Paqju'pe'k	Crooked Lake
Plisantek	Placentia (Note: this is a recent name. See *Ktaqmkuk – Across the Waters: Newfoundland Mi'kmaw Place Names* in References.)
Pmaqtin	Sacred Mountain, known in English as Mount Sylvester
Qa'qawejwe'katik	Crow Head (Note: this is a recent name. See *Ktaqmkuk – Across the Waters: Newfoundland Mi'kmaw Place Names* in References.)
Sapalqek	Through Hill
Sple'tk	River Exploits or Exploits River
T'maqanapskwe'katik	Pipe Stone Pond
U'nama'kik	Cape Breton Island
Wapeskue'katik	White Bear Bay

Place names given in English only:

Gaultois Island	Bonaventure
Pass Island	Bonavista Bay
Flat Bay River	Mount Clarence
Cold Springs Pond	Wilson's Lake
Random Sound	Little River

NUMBERS IN MI'KMAQ

1	ne'wt	6	asukom
2	ta'pu	7	l'uiknek
3	si'st	8	ukmuljin
4	ne'w	9	pesqunatek
5	na'n	10	newtiska'q

11	newtiska'q jel ne'wt	16	newtiska'q jel asukom
12	newtiska'q jel ta'pu	17	newtiska'q jel l'uiknek
13	newtiska'q jel si'st	18	newtiska'q jel ukmuljin
14	newtiska'q jel ne'w	19	newtiska'q jel pesqunatek
15	newtiska'q jel na'n	20	tapuiska'q

---

21 tapuiska'q jel ne'wt	**26** tapuiska'q jel asukom
22 tapuiska'q jel ta'pu	**27** tapuiska'q jel l'uiknek
23 tapuiska'q jel si'st	**28** tapuiska'q jel ukmuljin
24 tapuiska'q jel ne'w	**29** tapuiska'q jel pesqunatek
25 tapuiska'q jel na'n	**30** nesiska'q

40 newiska'q	**70** l'uiknek te'siska'q
50 naniska'q	**80** ukmuljin te'siska'q
60 asukom te'siska'q	**90** pesqunatek te'siska'q

100 kaskimtlnaqn	**600** asukom kaskimtlnaqn
200 ta'pu kaskimtlnaqn	**700** l'uiknek kaskimtlnaqn
300 si'st kaskimtlnaqn	**800** ukmuljin kaskimtlnaqn
400 ne'w kaskimtlnaqn	**900** pesqunatek kaskimtlnaqn
500 na'n kaskimtlnaqn	**1000** pituimtlnaqn

10,000	pituimtl naqnepikatun
1,000,000	kji-pituimtlnaqn

Chief Mi'sel Joe in search of pitcher plants, Miawpukek First Nation, July 2020. *(Photo courtesy of the authors.)*

Chief Mi'sel Joe, pitcher plants on the bog, Miawpukek First Nation, July 2020. *(Photo courtesy of the authors.)*

Chief Mi'sel Joe examining map of William Cormack's and Sylvester Joe's travels across the island of Newfoundland in 1822. *(Photos courtesy of the authors.)*

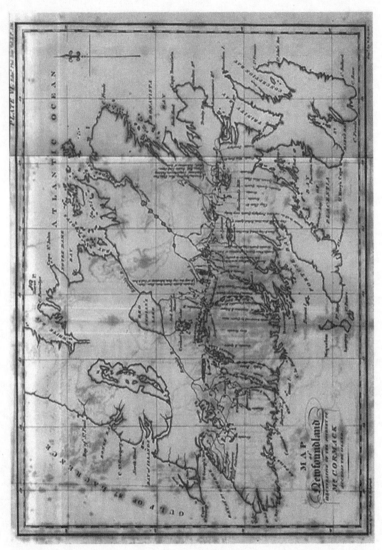

Guided by Sylvester Joe, Cormack's journey from Smith Sound, Trinity Bay, on September 5 1822, to St. George's Bay on November 4, 1822. *(Image from original edition of Cormack's journal.)*

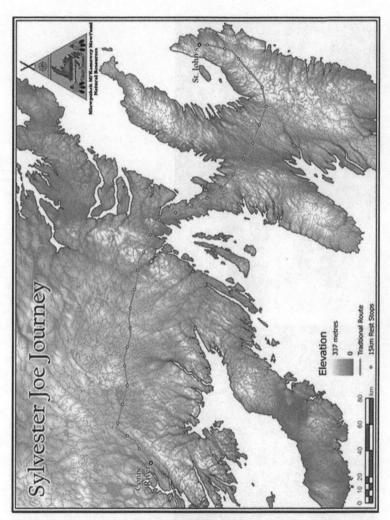

This map shows the traditional route used by Mi'kmaw people to travel across the eastern part of Newfoundland. This is likely the route Sylvester Joe used in 1822 to travel from Miawpukek to St. John's to meet Cormack.

(Map created by and courtesy of Greg Jeddore.)

Chief Mi'sel Joe in Scotland (2015) meeting with solicitor David J. Howat (deceased), who helped get things moving with the museum in Edinburgh.
(Photo courtesy of the authors.)

Chief Mi'sel Joe (2014) in front of the National Museum of Scotland.
(Photo courtesy of the authors.)

Aerial views of Mount Sylvester from a float plane, July 2017. *(Photos courtesy of the authors.)*

buttoned and belted round them, which looked neat and comfortable. Their caps were of mixed fur; they had not procured much fur for sale: only a few dozen marten, some otter, and musk-rat skins; of beaver skins they had very few, as beavers are scarce in the western interior, it being too mountainous for woods, except on the sheltered borders of some of the lakes. In the woods around the margin of this lake the Indian had lines of path equal to eight or ten miles in extent, set with wooden traps or dead-falls, about one hundred yards apart, baited for martens, which they visited every second day. They had two skin canoes in which they paddled round the lake to visit their traps and bring home their game. The Red Indian country, we were told, was about ten or fifteen miles northward of us, but at this time, as the mountaineer had likewise informed us, these people were all farther to the north, at the Great Lake, where they were accustomed to lay up their winter stock of venison. These people corroborated previous as well as subsequent inquiries respecting the number of their own, and of the other communicating tribes in the Island.

INDIAN TRIBES IN NEWFOUNDLAND IN 1822

I. MICMACS AND MOUNTAINEERS

All the Indians in the Island, exclusive of the Red Indians, amount to nearly a hundred and fifty, dispersed in bands, commonly at the following places or districts: St. George's Harbour and Great Codroy River on the west coast; White Bear Bay and the Bay of Despair on the south coast; Clode Sound in Bonavista Bay on the east; Gander Bay on the north

coast; and occasionally at Bonne Bay and the Bay of Islands on the north-west coast. They are composed of Micmacs, joined by some of the mountaineer tribe from the Labrador, and a few of the Abenaki from Canada. The Esquimaux, from Labrador, occasionally, but seldom, visit the Island. There are twenty-seven or twenty-eight families altogether, averaging five to each family, and five or six single men. They all follow the same mode of life, hunting in the interior, from the middle of summer to the beginning of winter in single families, or two or three families together. They go from lake to lake, hunting all over the country, working round one before they proceed to the next. They paddle along the borders, and the men proceed on foot up every rivule, brook, and rill, beavers being their primary object of search, as well as otters, martens, musk-rats, and every living thing; secondly, when the lakes are connected by rivers, or when the portages between them are short, they proceed in their canoes, or carry them with them; otherwise they leave them, and build others on arriving at their destination. The hunting season, which is in the months of September and October, being over, they repair to the sea-coast with their furs, and barter them for ammunition, clothing, tea, rum, etc.; and then most of them retire to spend the winter at or near the months of the large rivers, where eels are to be procured through the ice by spearing, endeavouring at the same time to gain access to the winter paths of the deer.

II. RED INDIANS. THE ABORIGINES. THE BEOTHUCKS

A great division of the interior of Newfoundland is exclusively possessed and hunted over by Red

Indian Tribes in Newfoundland in 1822 (top). Mount Sylvester, (below) the mountain that Cormack named after Sylvester Joe; Cormack refers to Sylvester as "My Indian".

(Photos courtesy of the authors, of pages from William Cormack's journal, A Journey Across the Island of Newfoundland in 1822.)

and other water-courses. It occurs of a globular structure on the verge of the savanna country westward of that branch of Clode Sound River which we crossed. The balls are round, and vary in size from a few inches to a fathom and upwards in diameter.

MOUNT SYLVESTER

In the whole of this savanna territory, which forms the eastern-central portion of the interior, there rises but one mountain, which is a solitary peak or pap of granite, standing very conspicuous about forty-five miles north from the mouth of the West Salmon River of Fortune Bay on the south coast. It served as an object by which to check our course and distance for about two weeks. I named it Mount Sylvester, the name of my Indian. The bed of granite, of which Mount Sylvester is a part, is exposed in a remarkable manner to the north-east of that pap near Gower lake. Here are displayed the features of the summit of an immense mountain mass, as if just peeping above the earth; huge blocks of red, pink, and gray granite, often very coarsely grained, and of quartz, compact and granular, lie in cumbrous and confused heaps, "like the ruins of a world," over which we had to climb, leap, slide, and creep. They sometimes lie in fantastical positions: upon an enormous mass of gray granite may be seen, as if balanced on a small point of contact, another huge mass of red granite more durable in quality, and this crowned by a third boulder. Their equilibrium invites the beholder to press his shoulder to them to convince him of his feebleness. These masses seem to be the remaining nodules or strata or beds that once existed here; the more

perishable parts having long since crumbled and disappeared, thus evincing the power of time.

Quartz rock, both granular and compact—the latter sometimes rose-coloured—occurs, associated with

Taken, by kind permission, from Millais' "Newfoundland and its Untrodden Ways."
MOUNT SYLVESTER—" A SOLITARY PEAK OR PAP OF GRANITE" (p. 46).

granite. On the summit of a low bristly ridge, formed principally of granular quartz, nearly half-way across the Island, are two large masses of granular quartz standing apart at the bottom, and nearly meeting at the top; seen at a distance, from the north or south they have the appearance of one mass with a hol

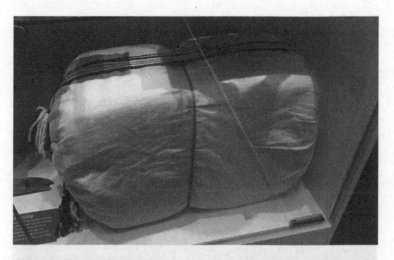

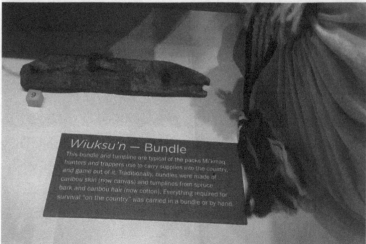

Wiuksu'n — Bundle

This bundle and tumpline are typical of the packs Mi'kmaq hunters and trappers use to carry supplies into the country, and game out of it. Traditionally, bundles were made of caribou skin (now canvas) and tumplines from spruce bark and caribou hair (now cotton). Everything required for survival "on the country" was carried in a bundle or by hand.

Chief Mi'sel Joe's bundle, on display at The Rooms. This type of bundle would have been used in Sylvester Joe's time and was used by Mi'kmaw guides and trappers up until the mid-1970s. The strap was made by Isabel Jeddore, Miawpukek First Nation, on a traditional loom.

(Photos courtesy of the authors.)

Chief Mi'sel Joe and his loom, which he made himself. They were used to weave bundle straps. *(Photo courtesy of the authors.)*

BOOK CLUB QUESTIONS

Why do you think the authors chose *My Indian* as the title of the book?

"My Indian" is how Cormack refers to his Mi'kmaw guide, Sylvester Joe, throughout his journal, *Narrative of a Journey Across the Island of Newfoundland in 1822*. The authors chose this title as a way of reclaiming the narrative. Much of Mi'kmaw history has been told though a colonial lens. Giving the book this title is a way of symbolically taking the name "My Indian" away from Cormack and giving it back to the Mi'kmaq of Newfoundland.

What is the significance of retelling the story of Cormack's journal, *Narrative of a Journey Across the Island of Newfoundland* in 1822 from Sylvester Joe's perspective?

This story has never been told from a Mi'kmaw perspective, only through Cormack's lens. Two hundred years ago, there was a different way of doing things. Cormack's interpretation of how to use the land and the things around him was different from that of the Mi'kmaq and the Beothuk who had been inhabiting the island for uncounted years. As natural environmentalists, they knew the land and all that it could offer, including food, clothing, shelter, and medicines.

What is the significance of the silver streak that both Sylvester and his grandfather had in their hair? How was it important to their relationship with the Beothuk people?

The Beothuk recognized Sylvester from his grandfather's time, when his grandfather was a captive of the Beothuk. This solidified the connection between the Mi'kmaq and the Beothuk people.

Why did Sylvester Joe travel to U'nama'kik/Cape Breton?

Sylvester Joe travelled to U'nama'kik/Cape Breton to find more Mi'kmaw people, to be educated about Mi'kmaw history, to meet the Grand Chief, to meet more Elders, and to talk about the vastness of the Mi'kmaw territory, which extended from Newfoundland all the way to what is now known as Atlantic Canada, Quebec, and even parts of the United States.

Why were there two ceremonies (one for the man, one for the woman) for one marriage?

Traditionally, there were always two ceremonies, one for the man and one for the woman. As with modern-day ceremonies, the groom does not see the bride on the wedding day. There were things for the wife to learn that only the women could tell her. For example, as his wife, she was the only one permitted to braid the man's hair. Becoming a wife is to become part of an elite group; she would be accepted into the circle. The wife of a warrior takes on a different role, with different responsibilities.

It would be the same with the man. He would have different roles as a husband. He would not only become a provider for his own family but would become part of an elite group of warriors and hunters, who would take on the responsibility of providing food for all the village. He would join the circle of men and Elders and would be groomed to become a leader and an Elder. He would now become part of an inner circle; a storyteller, a historian, and a spiritual guide for younger people. The men would continue to teach him to be humble and respectful around women, even more so now as a married man. When the two come together, the circle is complete.

Marriage and raising children were village obligations. It was frowned upon for young men to take women and then leave their families and go off on their own to raise their children. It was important for the families to be part of raising the children and passing on their spiritual belief and spiritual ceremonies. (Mi'sel Joe)

Why did Sylvester Joe go to the mountain with his grandfather? What did he learn?

Sylvester Joe went to the mountain with his grandfather to offer tobacco, to ask for prayers for good hunting and safety, and to ask for good luck for hunting and travel across the land. Sylvester learned that his grandfather spoke the Beothuk language and that he had lived with the Beothuk for two years and considered them friends.

When Sylvester meets Cormack, he tells Cormack that Sylvester is his church name. What does he mean by that?

When he was born, Sylvester was given the name Suliewey—Silver—because of the silver streak in his hair. In later years, the missionaries baptized him Sylvester, a Christian name.

Compare the similarities between Cormack's journal and Sylvester's travelling stick.

Cormack wrote in a book about his journey, and Sylvester put symbols on his stick to record each day of his journey. Sylvester's symbols included the form of a wikuom for campsites or a symbol for fire. Each ring on the stick represented a day's travel.

A journey stick was meant to be kept for one moon or longer. In both cases, the journal and the travelling stick were used to keep a record of their journey.

Why would Sylvester have used the word wikuom and not mamateek to describe the Beothuk homes?

Wikuom is the Mi'kmaw word, and at that time was the only word Sylvester would have known to use to describe 'home' or 'shelter'.

Sylvester's grandfather spent time living with the Beothuk when he was a child, and experienced part of their culture. What sort of things did he learn and do with the Beothuk?

Sylvester's grandfather learned some of the Beothuk language, played games that taught skills such as hunting, and was painted with red ochre, as the Beothuk were. He also learned from an Elder about how the Beothuk gave thanks for the gifts from the land.

Why did Mi'sel Joe, a Mi'kmaw Chief, decide to take action to repatriate Beothuk remains?

In Indigenous culture, remains are treated with respect. So this would have been important to all Indigenous people. There is also growing DNA evidence which confirms the oral history of intermarriage between the Mi'kmaq and the Beothuk. The Beothuk were seen by the Mi'kmaq as their brothers and sisters.

In what ways did Mi'kmaw people use balsam fir and birchbark? (Refer to Chapter 9)

The gum from the small blisters on balsam fir was used as a medicine to heal cuts. Tips of young balsam fir were eaten, and are known to be high in Vitamin C.

Birchbark had many uses: it was used to start a fire, for shelter, for building ocean-going canoes, and to make containers for bear fat, berries, or even for boiling water.

In Chapter 9, Cormack and Sylvester Joe talk about eggers. What is the difference between how Sylvester describes the European eggers and how the Mi'kmaq collected eggs?

Europeans were known to take all the eggs, and as a result destroyed colonies of birds, including the Great Auk. The Mi'kmaq did not take all the eggs out of the nest; they took only what they needed and left some eggs behind in each nest to ensure there would always be food for two or three generations.

Sylvester knew where the Beothuk were camped. What shaped his decision not to tell Cormack?

This decision was pre-determined by the Elders before Sylvester left Miawpukek in the spring of 1822. It was also influenced by his grandfather's friendship with the Beothuk.

What do you think happened to Sylvester between 1823 and 1828?

It is speculated that between 1823 and 1828, Sylvester went back to find and live with the Beothuk.

REFERENCES

Cuff, Robert. "Mi'kmaw women in the Newfoundland historic record." 2012

Cormack, William Epps. *Narrative of a Journey Across the Island of Newfoundland.* St. John's: Morning Chronicle Print, 1873.

Matthews, Michelle, and Dr. Angela Robinson. *Ktaqmkuk – Across the Waters: Newfoundland Mi'kmaw Place Names.* Qalipu First Nation: 2018.

Penney, Gerald. "Frank Speck and the Newfoundland Micmac: A Summary." In *Papers of the Twenty-first Algonquian Conference,* edited by William Cowan. Ottawa: 1990.

Speck, Frank G. *Beothuk and Micmac.* Volume in the series *Indian Notes and Monographs: A series of publications relating to the American Aborigines.* F.W. Hodge, editor. New York: Museum of the American Indian Heye Foundation, 1922.

Hewson, John. *Klusuaqney Wi'katikn: A Newfoundland Micmac Picture Dictionary.* Memorial University of Newfoundland: Department of Linguistics, 1978.

Repatriation News Links

'Stolen' Beothuk remains need to come home from Scotland, Mi'sel Joe says
CBC News · Posted: May 25, 2015 3:37 PM NT
https://www.cbc.ca/news/canada/newfoundland-labrador/stolen-beothuk-remains-need-to-come-home-from-scotland-mi-sel-joe-says-1.3086453

Ottawa backs request for return of Beothuk remains from Scotland. Government 'considers this matter to be of considerable importance,' heritage minister writes
Dean Beeby · CBC News · Posted: Aug 25, 2016 5:00 AM ET
https://www.cbc.ca/news/politics/beothuk-repatriation-mi-kmaq-newfoundland-1.3734419

Indigenous leaders unite for return of Beothuk remains, inclusion in MMIWG inquiry. Scottish museum said prior requests did not meet criteria, as there are no Beothuk descendants
Peter Cowan · CBC News · Posted: May 26, 2017 11:37 AM NT
https://www.cbc.ca/news/canada/newfoundland-labrador/indigenous-leaders-roundtable-1.4132582

Miawpukek chief leads effort to have Beothuk skulls returned from Scottish museum
July 13, 2017 Maureen Googoo
http://kukukwes.com/2017/07/13/miawpukek-chief-leads-effort-to-have-beothuk-skulls-returned-from-scottish-museum/

Remains of 2 Beothuk people to be transferred from Scotland to Canada. Authorities want move made 'as quickly as possible,' premier says
CBC News · Posted: Jan 21, 2019 12:04 PM NT
https://www.cbc.ca/news/canada/newfoundland-labrador/beothuk-remains-transfer-1.4986453

Beothuk remains returned to Newfoundland after 191 years in Scotland
https://www.cbc.ca/news/canada/newfoundland-labrador/beothuk-remains-returned-nl-1.5494373

Central Newfoundland Leaders want Beothuk Remains Returned to Red Indian Lake
https://www.thetelegram.com/news/local/central-newfoundland-leaders-want-beothuk-remains-returned-to-red-indian-lake-296144/

Remains of two of the last known Beothuk people returned to Newfoundland
APTN News Interview with Chief Joe
https://www.youtube.com/watch?v=qVDW9M-AjZs (Video)

Ministerial Statement Premier Dwight Ball Repatriation
March 11, 2020
https://www.facebook.com/watch/?v=716340765790461 (Video)
https://www.gov.nl.ca/releases/2020/exec/0609n03/